THE STORY OF LUMBER

This edition published 2025
by Living Book Press
Copyright © Living Book Press, 2025

ISBN: 978-1-76153-465-2 (hardcover)

978-1-76153-473-7 (softcover)

First published in 1912.

This edition is based on the 1912 printing by The Penn Publishing Company.

A catalogue record for this book is available from the National Library of Australia

THE STORY OF LUMBER

by

SARA WARE BASSETT

PLEASE NOTE

These books were written about 100 years ago and show the way people talked, thought, and acted back then. They tell the story of how resources like cotton, lumber, leather, and gold were developed—a process that depended on the hard work of many people. Sometimes the work was done by those who made the profits, and other times it was done by people who were not free, including enslaved individuals.

We know that some parts of these stories include ideas that we now understand to be hurtful and unfair. Our aim in republishing these books is not to support those old views but to share our history so we can all learn from it. By looking at the past, including its mistakes, we hope to learn important lessons that will help us create a kinder and fairer future.

We invite you to read these stories with an awareness of their time and to think about how far we have come—and how much work there is still to do.

Contents

To

DALLAS LORE SHARP

a lover of the woods,

this book is gratefully dedicated.

It gives me pleasure to acknowledge the kindness of the Hon. Gifford Pinchot who, because of his friendship both for the American Forest and for the American Boy, has generously placed at my disposal his "Primer of Forestry."

I am also very grateful to Mr. Fred H. Thompson, a member of the staff of the *Boston Post*, who had the good fortune to go down the Connecticut with the "Big 1911 Drive," and who has permitted me to make use of his experience.

S. W. B.

CHAPTER I

THE CLOUD AND ITS SILVER LINING

THE alert specialist looked critically at the boy before him, and shook his head.

"There will be no more books for you this year, young man!" he declared, smiling kindly. "You've been overdoing it, I'm afraid."

The boy closed his lips tightly, but disappointment and consternation were so evident in his face that the physician placed a hand upon his shoulder, saying cheerily:

"Why, my lad, most boys of your age would be but too glad to be cut loose from lessons. It is not as if you were to be on the shelf all your life. You'll take a year's rest and come back to study with those eyes of yours keener than ever."

Dick Sherman tried to smile.

"Eyes are not made of iron, boy. I'll be bound you've been working at mechanical drawing. Yes? I knew it! And the Greek alphabet? Yes. And mathematics? Yes—yes—yes. And your eyes, left weak from the measles you had recently, just kicked up and fussed at being overworked. Now you simply must give them a rest if you want them ever to do anything more for you. But remember, all the learning does not come from books; and your brain need not go to sleep while your eyes are on a vacation. You'll have to exercise them, and I'm going to get your father to send you off to some place where there are things worth learning, if they are not in books."

"But my class will go on without me," stammered Dick, wretchedly.

"I'm afraid so, sonny."

"And the fellows will make up the sophomore ball team, and I can't be on it."

"I suppose not."

"And I'll have to drop a year behind all my friends."

"Yes."

"And the school paper; and the basketball; and the hockey team—" Dick choked a little.

"Yes, I know just how hard it is."

"And the class will enter college without me—I'll never be able to catch up with them."

He turned away toward the window.

"It is hard luck," put in the older man, "but wouldn't you rather be a year late and take two good eyes with you to college than to go through life with no eyes at all?"

"Is it as bad as that?" Dick asked, soberly.

"That's about what it is. I know just how cut up you feel," said the doctor, warmly, "but I know, too, that you are enough of a man to buck up and make the best of it. You are not the only one disappointed. Your father and mother will be as sorry as you are. You can help make it easy for them by being brave yourself. This is the first big thing you've ever had to face, isn't it?"

"Yes, sir."

"Well, now's your chance to show what you're made of, and prove to your parents that you are worth all they have done for you."

Dick squared his shoulders.

"I'll try, sir."

"How old are you?"

"Fifteen."

"And here you are with a disappointment big enough for a full-grown man—that's a great compliment, Dick!"

The boy swallowed hard.

"You know it is no sort of a ship that can sail only in fair weather."

A faint smile crept over the averted face. Sailing was Dick's favorite sport. He held out his hand to the doctor and turning, faced him fairly.

"I'll do the best I can, sir," he answered, modestly.

As he walked out of the physician's office and started home, this resolve strengthened with every step. But that the disappointment was a crushing one, there was no denying. All through his freshman year in high school his eyes had bothered him, but he had fought along—foolishly, he now confessed—thinking they would soon be better. He had been trying to make the baseball team, and had worked hard to keep his place on the school paper. Then had come the hockey matches and skating. Study had, of necessity, been pushed to evening, or early morning, in a faint light where letters and figures were blurred and uncertain. Long ago he might have told his parents that his eyes ached, but he feared athletics would be cut off if he did so, or that he should be put into glasses—an annoyance which he did not feel he could bear.

But wearing glasses, and even the loss of all the ball teams in the world could not equal the calamity which had now fallen. Dick was man enough to argue that he had no one but himself to blame for this unlucky plight, and he therefore determined to bear it as bravely as he could.

So busy had he been with these arguments that he was surprised to find that, as he reached his conclusion, he was turning into his own front gate. He walked firmly up the steps and inserted his key in the lock of the front door, but before he could turn the latch the door swung open, and his mother met him.

Mrs. Sherman was a short, plump little woman, with a smile that smiled itself until you had to smile in return—at least Dick always did.

"Well, what did Dr. Haughton say, Dick? I suppose it is spectacles. Never mind, dear. They are not so much trouble as you think, after you get used to them. Besides, if you wear them all the time, you will always know where they are. Mislaying spectacles is the worst part of being tied to them."

While speaking she bustled about, helping the boy off with his coat, and glancing sharply into his face as he followed her into the sitting-room.

Mr. Sherman put down the paper as his son entered.

"What did Haughton say, Dick?" he asked, stooping to stir up the fire. "More spectacles in the family, I suppose."

"It is worse than that, father."

Struggle as he would, a tremor crept into Dick's voice.

"It is no books at all for a year, at least," he continued, more firmly. "You will have to turn me out to pasture, I think. Dr. Haughton says some way-up nerve has gone on a strike—he is going to telephone you about it—and he says that I've just got to stop everything until it is ready to come back to work."

In spite of the boy's attempt at control, his chin quivered.

Instantly both parents understood.

"Well, well, lad, it might have been much worse—try and think of that. Let us be thankful that a year can repair it all. Now we will think of something for you to do in the time; something you will enjoy, and that will keep you out of mischief."

Mr. Sherman rose and came toward Dick.

"Don't worry about it, my boy. We'll make some plans together, and perhaps it will come out better than you think."

"Dr. Haughton said," persisted Dick, honestly, "that if I had told you about my eyes last fall, or given up studying evenings—"

"Well, we are not all sages at fifteen," interrupted Mr. Sherman. "If you see you were foolish, remember the lesson and do differently next time."

"It is mighty good of you, father, not to rub it in," murmured Dick, gratefully. "You see, I was trying for the ball team; and there was basketball, hockey, and the school paper. I hated the thought of glasses—they are such a nuisance, and the fellows would guy so, and call me 'Professor.'"

"I understand, lad. It isn't all your fault, either. Your mother and I ought to have seen it ourselves."

During dinner nothing more was said about the matter, as it had always been a rule of the Sherman household that unpleasant subjects should not be touched upon at table. But when the three were once more in the library, and a blazing fire softened the chill of the April evening, the question was once more taken up.

The first suggestion was Mr. Sherman's office, but there was nothing Dick could do there which did not require the use of his eyes. Plan after plan was built up, only to be overthrown. Dick was becoming discouraged.

Two hours passed in fruitless debate, then suddenly Mrs. Sherman cried:

"I have the very thing for you, Dick! Why didn't I think of it before? How would you like to join Uncle Alf in the Canadian woods?"

Mr. Alfred Houston was a member of the Forest Commission having in its charge the inspection of vast tracts of timber land which stretched thousands of miles over the densely wooded portion of New Brunswick.

The instant Mrs. Sherman suggested the idea Dick's eyes brightened, and he started up eagerly.

"That would be the very thing, mother. I'd like it above everything else. May I go? Would Uncle Alf let me come?"

"A letter or two will settle that," Mr. Sherman answered, smiling at the boy's earnestness. "It certainly is a fine plan, if it can be carried out. You could learn a great deal about trees and lumbering, and you would be having a jolly good time, too. Only, if you go, Uncle Alf must give you some work, for you do not want to be an idler. There are many things you can do, or learn to do, which will help him. And you must promise, before you start, not to go into foolhardy adventures which will make you a care to him, as well as a worry to us."

"I'll give you my promise now, father," cried Dick.

Mrs. Sherman laughed.

"I think there will be time enough for that when the matter is settled," she said.

For a week Dick was all impatience, while letters sped between his home and the distant province. Surely there never was such a long week!

Then came a telegram, characteristic of Uncle Alf:

Will meet Dick at St. John station April twentieth and purchase his kit there.

Signed: ALF.

Dick threw his cap high into the air after reading the message. It seemed too good to be true! Greek alphabets, mathematics, the school paper, even the ball team, faded into nothingness in the face of this greater glory. Dick was surprised to find, in the two weeks preceding his journey, that many an envious lad of his acquaintance would gladly have cast books and bat to the burning to have been allowed to join the expedition. Only those who knew Dick best realized that his high spirits concealed a disappointment far more bitter than he permitted himself to confess.

"It is easily seen, Dick," observed Dr. Haughton, the oculist, jokingly, "that the trouble with your eyes was all a bluff. What you really wanted was to go off for a good time—and you are going to have it, too!"

Dick threw back his head, smiling a little gravely.

"It is not every foolish boy who finds such a pleasant punishment waiting for him, Doctor. I do not deserve it."

"You deserve it for being so plucky, and making the best of things," returned the big man, putting out his hand.

And then Dick knew that the sympathetic old physician understood.

CHAPTER II
INTO THE WOODS

MR. ALFRED HOUSTON proved he was no novice in purchasing the forest outfit necessary for a boy. When he and Dick embarked on the narrow branch railroad which was the nearest means of reaching the carry to McGregor Lake, a box of khaki suits, corduroys, flannel shirts, woolen stockings, heavy underwear, and low-heeled, water-proof boots accompanied them. These trappings did not interest Dick nearly as much as a pair of real moccasins made by Micmac Indians, or a short hunting knife, both of which his uncle had added to the equipment. The moccasins had gaudily beaded toes, and stout thongs for fastening; and the knife was in a case of deerskin, with a handle of roughly notched ebony. Dick had suggested a handle smoother in design, but Uncle Alf answered:

"The only way to choose a hunting knife is to consider the steel, and the grip you can get on the handle. Now try it for yourself."

Dick took up the one of smoother design, but clutch it as tightly as he would, the blade turned in his hand.

Then he tried the other.

Instantly he saw the advantage of the crisscross markings.

Besides the moccasins and knife, Dick had two other treasures presented to him by his father before leaving home— a fly-rod of split bamboo, and a light rifle.

What boy could have asked more?

And now as the train rattled, bumped and swayed, Mr. Houston talked of the woods, and his work there. Dick had an indistinct idea that his uncle's business was to "save the trees," but just why he should be traveling to a large lumber camp where he acknowledged they were to see them *cut*, Dick could not fathom. However, he listened, confident that his questions could wait.

They had ridden nearly two hours before the train stopped with an extra big bump and fish-rods, rifles, sweaters, and satchels were bundled out upon the platform of the very smallest station Dick ever had seen.

"Is this a place—a town?" he asked doubtfully.

"I don't wonder you asked, Dick," laughed his uncle. "Yes, this is Raven Brook, and here is Jake waiting for us. How are you, Jake?" to a bronzed woodsman before them. "This is my nephew, Dick Sherman. Just now he knows more about books than he does about trees, but we're going to change all that. I'll have you know, Dick, that Jake will be the best professor you can find. What he doesn't know about the woods isn't worth knowing. You've lived in the woods all your life, haven't you, Jake?"

The big fellow laughed with pleasure, holding out his hand to Dick.

"'Spect I was born in the crotch of a tree," he drawled.

He swung up the satchels in his hand, and led the way to the rear of the platform.

Here was another novelty for Dick!

The wagon awaiting them was in reality merely two oil-cloth-covered seats lashed upon a mud-caked running gear, with wheels very far apart. It did not look as if it could hold together, and Dick pictured with amusement the wheels journeying off, leaving the seats somewhere by the roadside. But he climbed in after his uncle, only to encounter another surprise.

After Jake had tied the luggage firmly to the back of the strange vehicle, he began winding the cords about Mr. Houston and the boy himself, fastening them securely to the back of the seat.

"Feel like a baby in a baby-carriage, I'll bet, Dick!" he chuckled. "Don't they ever tie folks where you come from?"

"Not when they are over four years old," answered Dick, laughing.

"Well, you'll be mighty glad of that rope later, I can tell you!"

"How is the carry after the storm?" asked Mr. Houston. "Pretty bad?"

"Washed out in places, sir. We'll have to fill in with boughs below the second bend. But it's a park compared with last year."

Jumping in, he gathered the lines into his hand and started.

"The men were out to Raven yesterday, sir, so we won't have to stop for provisions."

As the wagon made its way through the scattered settlement, Dick noticed that everyone they passed hailed his uncle with some word of greeting, and that Mr. Houston had a pleasant word for each. The town itself was the most dilapidated one the boy had ever seen. In fact, there was nothing to it but a few roughly boarded houses, a tiny church, and group after group of sawmills along the bank of the river.

As for being roped into the wagon—Dick could see no use in that, at all!

But after they had creaked for some time along the red clay of the level roads, they suddenly turned into a narrow, grass-ribboned path, and Jake shouted:

"Now, Mr. Dick Sherman, we are off for the woods!"

And they were off, as Dick soon found, on a roadway differing widely from the New York boulevards.

First, there was the mud! The heavy wagon wallowed along, splashing the ferns and brush beside the path. Mud caked on wheels, harness, and horse. Only the burlap and coarse blankets which covered the travelers and their luggage saved them from becoming unrecognizable.

Then came huge rocks which jutted into the road, and over which one wheel heaved, only to drop afterward into the mud with a tremendous "splosh." Dick and Uncle Alf shot from one end of the seat to the other, and Jake called:

"How 'bout that rope now, my lad?"

"It's all—right! I—never—could—stick—in—without—it!" panted Dick.

"Rough, crossing the Channel to-day, isn't it?" exclaimed Mr. Houston.

"If you call this like a park, I'm glad I did not come last year," cried Dick, as he and his uncle were crowded for an instant to one end of the seat, only to be jostled, the following second, to the other end.

Then came more splash, splash, splash, as the brown mud creamed about the wheels!

After this followed a new sensation.

They were out of the mud and bump, bump, bump, they went over a stretch of road made by placing even-sized tree trunks close together, from left to right across their path. This motion was far worse than the others.

"What do you call this?" gasped Dick, his voice being shaken out of him by the jar of the wagon.

"This is a corduroy road, my son," answered Jake, enjoying his distress. "Have these in New York State?"

"I—hope—n—n—n—o—t!"

It seemed as if that corduroy road had no end, but finally, it sloped gently downward, and the next Dick knew they were splashing through a brook, the clear water of which was almost level with the hubs of the wheels, and from which the wagon emerged "fresh as from the laundry," Jake said. Then they were off again and away through more mud; over more rocks; and jiggling across more stretches of corduroy.

Would they ever reach McGregor Lake? Dick wondered.

It was getting late and he was hungry. Moreover, he felt lame and sore from the continual roughness through which, for hours, he had been riding. But he made no complaint.

Probably his uncle was tired too; Dick thought he must be. The older man, however, chatted as they drove along, calling attention to the gigantic pines—straight as arrows—which towered over their heads. Dick had never seen such trees!

"That is where we get our masts, Dick, and our telegraph

They Were Crossing A Stream

poles," Mr. Houston remarked proudly. "You have no handsomer trees than those—even in your state."

"No, sir. They are the biggest ones I ever saw."

"Those saplings must be thinned, Jake," continued Mr. Houston, pointing to a group of young spruces.

Again Dick wondered how Uncle Alf could be working to "protect the forest" if he thus proposed cutting and thinning the trees, and this time he was on the point of asking when *jar, jar, jar,* they went rumbling over more corduroy. This time it was even a worse rattle than they had met before, and, looking ahead, Dick saw they were crossing a stream by means of a log bridge. The trees of which this was made were but little longer than the wagon was wide, and every moment there seemed a good chance that a wheel might run off the edge.

"Nice bath we'd get if it did," he thought to himself, as he glanced down into the water.

"But it won't," Uncle Alf said aloud, "so don't worry."

Dick started.

"I don't see how you knew," he laughed, "but I *was* thinking that very thing. I should not mind the swim, but I do not like being tied in."

Mr. Houston, meantime, turned critically in his seat, examining the bridge.

"Who laid this roadway, Jake?" he demanded sharply. "The trees are undersized. This sort of thing won't do, you know."

"Peter's gang cut the spruces, sir."

"Well, Peter's gang will have to stop slashing into saplings, or there will be trouble. You see, Dick, they have cut small, straight trees that should have been left to grow into big fellows, like those we saw just now. You know what it is to have ripe fruit?"

"Yes, sir."

"Well, trees are ripe for gathering, as fruit is. When they get their growth they should be cut, to make room for younger trees. But what will happen if you cut them before they are ripe?"

"You won't get such big trees," answered Dick, promptly.

"And will you get so much money for smaller trees?"

"I suppose not, sir."

"And by and by, when you have cut all these small trees and want big ones, where will you be?"

"Why, there won't be any big ones."

His face brightened, for he began to see what "protecting the forest" meant.

"And suppose," went on his uncle, "that you cut all the little and big trees at once, will you have any to cut next year, or the year after?"

"No, sir. But I never thought of it before."

"Jake and I have thought of it, though, eh, Jake?" queried Mr. Houston. "And that, Dick, is what we are doing at McGregor Lake. We are not cutting the trees ourselves, but we are trying to show these short-sighted woodsmen what to cut."

"I see, sir. And then they cut the trees you tell them."

"That's just the rub, my boy. Some of them do not want to cut the trees we tell them. They do not know enough to see it is the best way in the end. So Jake and some of the others are trying to help me teach them. I shall expect you to do some teaching, too."

"But I don't know anything about it—I'd help you, if I did."

"Jake and I mean you shall know."

"And these are some of the lessons that are not in books," thought Dick. "Well, I have learned something already."

They had now jogged far into the forest, churning through more mud and over more boulders. Dusk was gathering and it was very still. From out of the wood came the chill breath of the pines, prompting Dick to wriggle into his sweater. Then he listened. Far off he could hear voices and snatches of song, while the faint odor of a fire drifted toward them.

"It's the camp, Dick," Mr. Houston said. "I am sure you are glad. I am! Do you suppose you are good for a potato and a bit of bacon?"

"Two potatoes, sir, I think," returned the boy.

"On a pinch, they might find two for you," chuckled Jake.

Meanwhile the voices came nearer, and in a moment the horse plunged through brakes and brush, and stood beside a group of rough pine shanties, on the shore of a large lake. Many men hurried hither and thither, greeting Mr. Houston; nodding to Dick; untying the travelers and their luggage; and unharnessing the horse. Then Dick followed his uncle into a small lean-to.

At one end of the little cabin was a platform slanting toward the center of the room, and covered thickly with fresh pine boughs.

"That's our bunk, lad."

Dick nodded.

Had his uncle proclaimed that they were to sleep standing upright, he believed he could have done it.

This certainly was real camping! Already he was anxious to be free of his city suit and inside some of the rougher clothes crowding the corded box in the corner. But his uncle left him only time enough to drop the luggage, hurrying him off to the cook-house. Here on a long wooden table built crudely of timber and surrounded by long benches, Dick found a tin plate, flanked by fork, dipper, and spoon of like metal. And by the light of a lantern he ate two large potatoes, heaped about with slices of sizzling bacon.

Then he remembered vaguely dipping water from a bucket into a tin basin on a shelf outside the cabin door; bathing sleepily; tumbling into woolen pajamas; and then rolling himself in the coarse blankets upon the pine boughs. From somewhere came dancing firelight and the crackling of logs. Then, amid the great silence of the forest, he heard only the borers, working ceaselessly in the rotting timber of the lean-to. Afterward even this ceased, and Dick Sherman slept.

CHAPTER III

THE FIRST SHOT

HEN Dick opened his eyes amid his new surroundings the next morning, it took him a moment to remember where he was. Then the chilly spring breeze, blowing stiffly from the lake, brought him to his senses. His uncle was already gone, only a hollow in the pine boughs beside the boy marking the spot where he had slept.

Dick sprang up. He found the tin basin and bucket inside the cabin door, and after a dash of cold water, he hurried into a flannel shirt and corduroys. Round his neck he knotted a scarlet handkerchief, as he had seen Jake do, and running his leather belt through the case of his hunting knife, he pulled his sweater over his head, and started for the cook-house.

Although it was scarcely light, the camp was already astir, and as the boy dropped down on the bench beside his uncle, he was not a little mortified to find that most of the lumbermen had already gone, and that he himself was the latest comer. Jake and about fifteen others were finishing salt pork and flapjacks.

"You did pretty well, my boy," Mr. Houston said. "I hadn't the heart to wake you early after your jaunt over the carry. How are you—black and blue?"

"I didn't stop to look, sir, but I guess not."

Jake grinned.

"I reckon you'll do, lad," he declared, tipping some condensed milk into his tin dipper of coffee.

"Chip off the old block, eh?" called a burly fellow from the end of the table.

Dick glanced at him.

It was the handsome, half-insolent face of a young French Canadian, whose skin was darkened to a rich walnut by exposure to the weather. A shirt that had once been red, but had now mellowed to deep pink, strained across his broad shoulders. There was something in the sweep of hair shading his brow, in the black eyes, in the very careless knot of the handkerchief about his neck, which carried fascination with it.

"You'll never catch your uncle doin' any fussin'," drawled on the woodsman. "Whatever is good enough for the boys is good enough for him."

"We're all lumber-jacks here, aren't we, Silver?" Mr. Houston replied, smiling.

"Is that his real name?" Dick whispered.

"Yes, Silver La Rue," returned Mr. Houston in the same low tone. "Rather musical, isn't it?"

The boy nodded. "Where are the other men?" he asked. "There were hundreds here last night."

"They have gone up the Sherwood trail to lay a logging

road; but there were not hundreds of them, only about twenty-five. The camp is small now because the rivermen are out with the drive. The drive is getting the logs down the river, you know," Mr. Houston added, as he saw the puzzled look on Dick's face.

Dick nodded.

"You see, uncle, I'm pretty raw," he laughed.

"Every process is a study in itself," Mr. Houston answered. "I did not expect you to know about something you had never looked into. You'll learn. The best way is to ask, every time you hear a term used that you do not understand. Don't be ashamed—pitch in, and find out. Now this morning we are going up the Eagle trail to look over the trees. Are you ready for a six or eight mile tramp, Dick?"

"Try me!"

"We're off, then."

As he rose, Mr. Houston called to the men:

"You fellows get your axes and stuff, and come along."

Drawing on an old slouch hat, he turned down a narrow, beaten trail, and Dick, who trotted behind, noticed that the trees at each side of it were notched, or "blazed" at regular intervals.

"I warn you now, Dick," Mr. Houston called over his shoulder as they went along, "never wander from the blazed trees when you are in the woods. The better a man knows the forest, the more he realizes the danger of getting off the trail. Remember that—it is the biggest law of a woodsman."

Before they had gone far Dick realized that his uncle certainly merited the title of "woodsman." He covered the ground with rapid swing, never wasting the energy to step upon a fallen tree-trunk if he could step over it. His pace slackened not one whit. The boy pattered behind him in his moccasins, quite breathless.

Once in the woods it was far warmer than on the lake shore, even though in the hollows under the hemlocks patches of snow still lingered.

"We are off in a different world, you see," observed Mr. Houston. "The forest has its own plants, which will grow nowhere else; its population of animals; it makes its own floor; and it has a climate of its own, too."

"It certainly is warmer here than near the lake," Dick replied. "I thought it would be colder—it is always colder in summer, when you get into the woods."

"The trees check the sweep of wintry wind, you know. Often persons in exposed localities leave the forests which shelter them as windbreaks to protect either dwellings, or other trees. Acres of timber are frequently protected in this way, for heavy gales are one of the worst enemies to the trees—especially if their branches are laden with snow. Another reason the forest is warmer in winter is because then its floor is frozen, and cannot absorb the heat from the air, as it does in summer."

"Its floor!"

"Yes, as I said, the forest makes its own floor—you know that. Think a moment."

"You mean the leaves and pine-needles that fall on it?" asked Dick.

"Of course. And the decaying plants and wood, besides. All these fall gently until the porous covering is made on which we are now walking."

"But," burst in Dick, "I never thought that all that mushy stuff was any use!"

"Oh, my!" laughed his uncle, "we'd be in a very sorry state without the mushy stuff, for the rain and melting snows filter through it, and run off into the brooks, thus keeping the streams filled. Now, if you cut down all the trees—" he paused.

"I suppose the forest floor, as you call it, would be sun-baked—dry up—harden."

"Right again! Then the water would drain quickly off its surface into the streams, causing them to overflow. Freshets and floods would follow so long as this great torrent of water continued. Afterward the streams would be dry until another rain."

"Then the forest floor holds back the water and deals it out slowly," Dick said.

"Precisely. And the trees at the heads of the streams help also by preventing the snows from melting too quickly, and by keeping the ground there moist. Of course you know already that the roots of trees hold the soil together, and aid in stopping landslides on the mountainsides."

Dick nodded.

"But you have not yet told me why the forest is cooler in summer," he ventured thoughtfully.

"Well, not only does its floor absorb the heat and thus cool the air, as I mentioned, but the forest influences both the moisture and the wind. The leaves of the trees contain much water, and when the sunlight reaches them they give off vapor—"

"Like a teakettle!" interrupted Dick.

"Yes, the idea is the same, although we cannot see the vapor in this case. The leaves drink in the sunshine and warm air, and give out a cool moisture. Beside that, the tree itself takes from the air certain elements that help it to grow. These elements are stored away in the wood, to make heat in future; later, when we burn the wood, we set those elements free. So we are correct in saying roughly that the tree takes from the air just the amount of heat which it gives out when burning."

"I never knew that!" Dick murmured.

"Now," continued Mr. Houston, "just as fast as the air is cooled by the tree and its leaves, it settles heavily to the ground and the hot air, that is lighter, rises into the tree tops, to be made cool. Afterward the cool air from the forest drifts off into the country, to refresh the land. Add to this that the branches are constantly keeping the air in motion, and you will readily understand that trees have a genuine influence upon the climate of the countries where they grow. Often, too, the sun gathers moisture from their tops, or crowns, just as it does from the seas and lakes, and we have more rain in consequence."

"Why, I shouldn't think anyone would ever cut down a tree, when it does these things for us," observed Dick, a good deal awed.

"Well, anyone certainly ought to think twice before he does it," laughed his uncle.

"And we are going to help teach the men all this!" mused the boy.

"Yes, and much more if we can, but—hush!"

Without warning Mr. Houston suddenly crouched behind a thicket of black birch, drawing Dick beside him.

"Don't breathe!" He pointed excitedly down the trail.

He Pointed Excitedly Down The Trail

Dick looked.

Out into the clearing swung a large buck, which paused a moment to sniff the twigs overhead—then stood motionless, listening.

Dick's hand was on the new rifle that he had insisted upon bringing.

Mr. Houston's hand also went out toward the gun, then he drew it back and nodded to Dick.

"Aim at his shoulder! Above the belly, if you can! Steady!" he whispered.

There was a flash and a report!

The deer sprang into the thicket, then wavered.

There was another shot—this time from some other rifle than Dick's.

Jake bounded down the trail.

"A good shot of yours, young one!" he cried. "You struck him, and I guess I finished the job. Come on!"

Wild with excitement, Dick raced after Jake.

Sure enough, the creature was stretched lifeless upon the ground.

"McGregor Camp will have a let-up from beans and salt pork for a while," Jake said, thrusting his hunting knife into the chest of the deer to bleed him. "You struck him in the flank, Dick."

He pointed to the wound. "Pretty good, for a first try!"

"Yes, indeed," echoed Mr. Houston, who had just come up. "I'm proud of you!"

By this time the other men had joined the group.

The big red-shirted man, whom they called Silver, slapped the boy on the shoulder.

"Many a man older than you, youngster, does no better than that," he said.

"I guess it was an accident," laughed Dick nervously—he was still too excited to be calm. "I did not dream I'd really hit. I never could do it again!"

"You've a good aim, and a steady hand. Take some lessons of Jake, here—he seems to know everything there is to know about shooting," sneered Silver, disagreeably.

If Jake detected the sneer, he paid no attention to it. He simply gave Silver a quick glance, then turned to Mr. Houston.

But in that instant Dick discovered something.

Jake had an enemy—Silver, the red-shirted leader of Peter's gang!

What could be the trouble?

Why should anyone hate Jake—the best-natured fellow in the whole camp?

There was no time now to work out the mystery.

Instead, he knelt on the ground and helped Jake and two of the men tie the deer's feet together, while others went off to cut a stout pole on which to swing their prize, and carry it back to the camp.

As the men set out, bearing the buck on their shoulders, Mr. Houston called:

"Are you going on with us, Dick, or would you rather go back with the deer?"

"Oh, I'm going on, Uncle Alf. I'd never turn back now—I might miss something."

Everybody laughed.

They started on.

"Little Toby, one of the Indians up at Sherwood Camp, is a

great one at making moccasins, Dick," said Jake, as they went along. "We'll have you a fine buckskin pair out of that deer's hide. And speakin' of moccasins—I hope to goodness you've got inner soles in those you have on now. If you haven't, you'll get blisters on your feet, and be done up by the time we come back. Moccasins ain't for the tenderfoot, you know."

Dick smiled.

"Yes, I've got in the soles—Uncle Alf made me. I thought it was silly, and I did not want to wear them, but I see now he was right."

"Better wear them until you get toughened up a bit," advised Jake.

Dick found Jake, as Mr. Houston had predicted, a most interesting woodsman. He pointed out to the boy the tracks of a raccoon, telling him how that strange little creature can make himself into a ball when pursued, and roll along the ground to the foot of a tree, only to dart up its trunk with lightning speed. He told Dick, too, how the animal never eats food which it has not washed, even though it is forced to drag it a long way in order to reach water. Then they discussed "coon" shooting and by that time they found themselves at the far end of Eagle trail, where Jake pointed out to Mr. Houston one of the blazed boundaries of the lot they had come to look over.

With the aid of a compass and Jake's notes, they located the others.

"As you men know," said Mr. Houston, "we can follow any one of three plans when we cut these trees: The first plan is to decide just how many big pines, spruces, etc., we will take out each year. The second way is to fix our limit at so many feet—board measure, of course—and cut just that amount. Or—the last way—we can let Dalton and Company decide how many years they want to cut this timber, and divide it up into that number of parts, cutting over one part each year. That is called the yield by area, and is the method they, together with most lumbermen, have been following. Now Dalton and Company have control of this land for a long stretch of years and they feel, as I do, that with careful cutting there will be an endless supply of timber ahead of them."

He stopped a moment, eying the men.

"In the past," he continued firmly, "you fellows have done a lot of injury to the young trees. No care has been taken to protect them, or foster their growth. All that sort of thing has got to stop. You have been getting out your lumber to the ruin of the property. I don't say you have meant this. It is because you have not known better. Now we are going to learn better, and after we have learned, woe to the man who does not follow what is taught him!"

Mr. Houston smiled, but there was no question that he intended to carry out the principles for which he had come.

The men knew his iron will—they had worked under him too long not to have encountered it—and they respected its force. Silver had summed up Mr. Houston by saying:

"He's awful pleasant 'til you get too pleasant—then he ain't pleasant at all!"

But despite the firmness of his hand on the men, there was no greater idol in the camp than Mr. Houston. When making his rounds of inspection for the Forest Commission his criticism was severely just, but kind. He had a word of greeting for every one—from the cookee to the rivermen.

And now that he had come to McGregor Camp to lay out the management of Dalton and Company's timber, his task was greatly lightened by having the good-will of the men. Such a task, at best, was not easy. No one realized better than Mr. Houston himself the difficulty of explaining to experienced lumbermen the principles of forest management which he intended to pursue. He knew they would call it nonsense and obey him merely because they must, rather than because they believed in what he was doing. What he wished to win was their belief—to make them see his method was such a wise one that they would follow it of their own accord even though he was not there to enforce it.

"Hereafter," continued he, "we will take nothing under ten-inch diameter; and when, here and there, a big tree protects seedlings or saplings from the light, we shall leave it. That makes you sniff, Silver. But isn't it better to have a bit smaller yield and guarantee that yield will hold out for years, than to ruin our future prospects with a big drive this year?"

Silver grunted, unconvinced.

"I ain't onto these new-fangled ideas, sir," he answered. "I've been a lumber-jack near twenty years, and haulin' logs is—is just haulin' logs to me. But whatever you say goes."

"Well, Silver, scores of times you must have seen hemlocks growing up in the shadow of white pines, waiting to take their places."

"Yes, sir."

"That's because the hemlock seedlings can live in heavy shade. But reverse the case—put a pine in the shade of a big hemlock, and the pine will die, because it must have the light. It is so with all trees. Certain of them can bear the shade, certain of them cannot. If the trees that need light can't get it they will fight to reach it."

"Course I know a white pine will shoot up miles for light," said Silver, slowly. "I know that. An' I know, too, all trees squabble for water, an' for room to get their branches out."

"That's so, Silver," Mr. Houston replied. "Now we are going to watch the young trees, and do for them the thing which will make them grow best. If they need shelter from wind, or if they want light, or room to stretch themselves, as we cut we are going to cut carefully enough to give them that particular thing. We may have to sacrifice something to do it, but we want to bring up this property for Dalton and Company until it is the best managed timber land in the country. Dalton has been good to you men—show him what you can do for him."

There was a little rustle of approval. Some of the men rubbed their hands and nodded. Others spoke in whispers to those beside them.

Dalton and Company had always been generous with their men. Many a one had drawn his pay when disabled, had been given time off if his family were sick, and had received money for extra work. Most of their workers had been in their employ for years and were proud of the fact. Loyalty is one of the logger's best qualities.

"I s'pose," Silver muttered, "Dalton and Company have a right to do as they please. Mr. Dalton can afford to. But—"

"But what?" questioned Mr. Houston.

"But I'll bet it does not work out. In the end he will lose money."

"Don't be too sure of that, Silver," Mr. Houston replied, turning away.

The men now formed in a long line at the boundary of the timber tract and, keeping as nearly even as possible, proceeded slowly across it, marking with a peculiar cross the trees Mr. Houston and Jake designated to be cut the coming winter. Then having explained and started the work it was left with a foreman to be carried out, and Jake, Mr. Houston, and Dick returned to the camp.

There the boy found one of the woodsmen boiling the brain of the buck they had killed in order that the liquid might be used in removing the hair from the hide, which had already been taken off.

"Toby will make you a fine pair of high moccasins out of that hide, Dick. See what a big one it is. They got it off whole. Those beaded things of yours are prettier to look at, but they are not good for much in woods like these."

Dick glanced down at his feet.

"There are not as many beads on them as there were this morning, Jake," he laughed.

"Well, there will be less after the next tramp—if that's any comfort to you," Jake answered drily, stretching the deer's hide over a pole to dry.

CHAPTER IV

THE LOST TRAIL

ICK had not been a week at McGregor Lake before he was surprised at the ease with which he dropped into camp life.

He made the acquaintance of Lutz, the German cook, and so entirely won his heart by helping him turn flapjacks that ever after he was in peril of having his digestion ruined by doughnuts and hot ginger-bread. The cookee, as Lutz's helper was called, was a young boy named Raoul, who was about Dick's own age, and who proved to be Silver's younger brother. Now and then Raoul found leisure to sit outside the cook-house door with Dick, and as the two whittled at toy boats or peeled birch bark, the Canadian told many a tale of the woods.

But as Raoul had to chop all the fuel for the camp; keep the fires going; clean both the small cabins and the large one where the men slept on long rows of bunks; bring water and fresh balsam boughs for bedding; and help Lutz prepare the meals, he had short hours for play. Dick found, however, that he could assist in this work. Gradually he dropped into the way of performing a little round of duties each morning and night and was astonished to discover that these self-imposed tasks made him feel much more a part of the McGregor life. He, too, now had a share in being useful. Moreover, he also won time for Raoul to go off with him. The young Frenchman shared Silver's charm, but lacked his recklessness, and therefore Mr. Houston felt him the safest of guides in the woods. He had gathered a fund of miscellaneous knowledge about beavers, hedgehogs, loons, and canoe-making which astonished Dick, making him feel very ignorant despite his years of schooling. On the other hand, Dick discovered that occasionally he could tell the forest-bred lad stories of war-ships, motor-cars, and air-ships, none of which Raoul had ever seen.

Together the two tramped up the trail to Sherwood Camp, fifteen miles higher on the ridge of Blue Mountain—another of Dalton and Company's camps. And once, when Raoul could be spared, they walked to Eagle Camp, at the far end of the Eagle trail, and spent the night there, carrying a message from Mr. Houston to the foreman in charge.

Dick was pleased to find that there were many ways in which he could be of use to his uncle. The days filled up and were not half long enough, and when he dropped onto the balsam boughs at night it was only to find that before he knew it, it was morning again.

Every few days somebody went out to Raven Brook for provisions, bringing letters back to Dick from his parents and the fellows at home. His mother missed him; his father hoped he was improving his time; the boys wrote that the ball team had won ten games and stood in line for the championship; that the school paper was booming; that Chase was to be captain of the football team the coming year. The little pangs which these letters caused at first gradually became fainter and fainter until, as life at McGregor became busier, they disappeared altogether and Dick was amazed to discover one day that he really cared next to nothing who was captain of the football team. The world seemed so big, and there was so much to learn—all those wonderful things which, as Dr. Haughton had told him, were not in books.

Dick had taken his uncle's advice and made himself a veritable question-box. With pleasure the men listened to his queries and answered them, for they were never idle questions. If, after careful thinking, he did not understand a thing, then he asked.

It was in this way that he had learned that trees are classed as *tolerant* and *intolerant*—tolerant trees being those that can live in the shade, and intolerant those that cannot. On talking further with his uncle Dick also found out that trees three feet high or less are called seedlings; those from three to ten feet, saplings; from four feet high to a diameter of four inches, large saplings; from four inches to eight inches in diameter, small poles; from eight inches to twelve inches in diameter, large poles; from one to two feet in diameter, standards; and those two feet or more, veterans. All these measurements, Mr. Houston told him, must be taken the height of a man's chest from the ground. Dick amused himself classifying the trees as in kindergarten, primary, grammar, high school, or college, and it was not long before, when he saw them growing, he could actually put them in the class where they belonged. This knowledge, and the understanding that a college class of ripe trees must "graduate" each year, made him comprehend perfectly his uncle's system in marking the trees for cutting.

"Don't you see, Silver," he explained, "Uncle Alf can't let all the trees graduate this year—they are not all ready and besides, if he did, who would be left to graduate next year?"

Silver looked thoughtful.

"There's some sense in that, Dickie," he replied. "It all seemed trash to me at first. Our gang has always cut a district over clean and taken every foot of timber growing on it. Of course we left it bare as your hand, but that wasn't our lookout. We leased it to cut, and we cut it! Afterward, it went back to the state, and if it lay idle until the trees grew on it again, it was nothing to us. Your uncle's plan is to cut less timber, and it looks to me as if Dalton and Company will lose money by it. But if your uncle saves out small trees that will grow so he'll get a crop each year, I can see sense in his plan. Instead of having one big cutting, he will have lots of cuttings. It seems as if it ought to work, only before I swallow it whole, I'm going to see it work. If it does, I'll take off my hat to your uncle. I will say that I never yet knew him to be wrong."

And Silver was as good as his word. He worked faithfully, furthering Mr. Houston's scheme by every means in his power.

Gradually spring wore on. Lumber roads were laid ready for the winter's hauling; maple sugar was boiled for use in the camp; and the buds on the trees slowly ventured forth, clothing the bare forest with a dress of freshest green.

When the ice was fairly out of the streams, Dick began anxiously to rig his fly-rod for trouting. Raoul owned a steel rod, and knew every brook that flowed into McGregor but, much as he loved the sport, he was too busy for long tramps.

"I don't see why I can't go alone, Uncle Alf," said Dick at last, impatient at waiting day after day for someone to fish with him. "I know the woods pretty well now, and I would keep near the trail."

"It is never safe for a man to go off by himself in this wilderness, my boy," Mr. Houston answered. "A score of things might happen. You be patient until we finish marking those trees in the Sherwood lot, and then I'll send Jake or Silver with you—they deserve a holiday; or, perhaps, I myself can get away for a trip. I am sure I should like to."

So Dick waited, but the day never seemed to come. Mr. Houston was wanted, or Silver was wanted, or Jake was wanted.

What did come was an army of small black flies that made wretched the days of the sturdiest woodsman. Work in the timber was torment, and night was worse. Every evening the men burned before the shanty doors smudges of peat and damp moss, and everybody was glazed over with ointment. The long buckskin moccasins which little Toby had made for Dick reached beyond his knickerbockers and proved a great protection.

But it would have taken more than black flies to quench Dick's ardor for fishing. Eagerly he fingered his rod and waited.

Of course he had fished some, for, from an old punt, he had caught dozens of yellow perch from the lake.

But this was not really sporty fishing.

At last, one afternoon when the camp was deserted, he could stand it no longer. He came out of the cabin with his rod and basket, and Raoul, who had heard Mr. Houston's orders, hailed him in astonishment.

"Where on earth are you going, Dick?"

Dick started. He had hoped to slip away without being seen.

"Oh, I'm just going up Sherwood way a bit—not far, you know—and I shall not go off the trail. I just want to cast a few times into that brook up there."

"Well, you just better not go wandering off anywhere. You know what your uncle told you."

Dick flushed irritably.

"I'm not going wandering off—you needn't worry. I should think you all took me for a baby three years old."

He sauntered down the trail.

Long, cool shadows flecked the path, spangling it with dancing patches of shade and sunshine. There was not a sound except the breaking of twigs under his feet, as he stopped now and then to gather delicate leaves of checkerberry, or to examine a group of fragile white Indian pipes.

He tramped along with the steady, even jog which he had learned from those accustomed to the woods, and soon he caught the trickling of the brook that crossed the Sherwood trail and slipped down toward McGregor Lake. This was Robin Hood Brook which he had come out to seek.

His plan was to fish up the tiny stream until he reached the place where it forked. He remembered hearing Silver say that somewhere near here, in a deep pool beneath overhanging rocks, were the largest trout to be found anywhere about.

If he could only catch one of those trout!

So off the trail and into the thicket dashed Dick.

Great brakes, waist-high, washed past him as he went; and often twigs of black birch whipped back, striking him across the face with stinging cuts. At every step he stirred up clouds of flies and insects. Still he followed the brook, cling-ing to its overgrown bank; wading cheerfully up to his knees through its dancing waters; or jumping from stone to stone. More than once some rock which looked solid tipped, caus-ing him to lose his footing; and many a moss-grown boulder was carpeted with velvet so smooth that the boy was forced to slip back into the stream to retain his balance. To cast a fly was well-nigh impossible, for overhead the trees interlaced, tangling his line upon their swaying branches.

"I'll have to give up casting," he declared at last, as he reeled in the silken cord. "I'll let out only a little line, put a worm on instead of a fly, and see what will happen."

What happened happened very quickly!

A great speckled four-pounder rose to the wriggling worm the instant it touched the water, and a few moments later lay gasping on the bank.

Dick danced with joy!

This was the sort of thing he had been fretting to do, and see how easy it was. Nothing had happened to him. He was still near the trail. Surely now his uncle, who was far too careful of him, would see how mistaken and silly he had been.

"It isn't as if I had gone far," Dick argued. "I guess he won't mind this little trip. Besides, when we give him these trout for supper to-night it will be such fun to hear him wonder where they came from."

He put fresh bait on the hook and dropped the line again.

Another trout rose—not quite so large, but a good fish, nevertheless.

The lad's blood was up.

He Put Fresh Bait On The Hook

He tried further along the stream, still searching for the famous deep pool.

Occasionally the brook divided, but nowhere were those great boulders that Silver had described. Following each time the larger fork of the stream, Dick sped on.

It was not until he raised his head to listen to a strange sound in the trees that he discovered it was growing dark.

How long had he been fishing, he wondered.

He looked at his watch.

It was after seven o'clock!

"Why, I must be miles from McGregor!" he exclaimed. "What on earth will they think has become of me? It's right about face, and sprint, too. I shall be awfully late as it is."

Quickly as possible he took his rod apart, then started back down the brook as he had come.

But returning was not as easy as he had expected, for not only was he tired, wet, and hungry, but twilight gathered fast. Search as he would, he did not reach the trail, and still the darkness came on. In the dim light he stumbled along, creeping at a snail's pace lest he lose his footing.

Then suddenly terror came upon him—*he could no longer see!*

But he persisted.

If he could but keep to the brook, following its sound, he would come out on McGregor Lake, a few miles to the west of the camp. Once on the lake shore he would kindle a bonfire which they could not fail to see from the Point, and they would come with a canoe and get him.

So on he struggled, the trickling of the stream his only guide.

Then, entirely without warning, he stepped off the edge of something high, crashed into the bracken below, and knew nothing more!

When he came to himself, a great flickering glare blazed among the trees.

Then out of the vagueness came voices—Jake's and Silver's.

His face was wet and they were bending over him.

"We've found you, laddie, thank heaven! Are you hurt?"

It was Silver speaking.

Afterward someone lifted him, oh, so gently, steadying him with a strong arm. That was Jake.

And there were other voices, and Raoul and some of Peter's gang were holding flaring pine-knots, and taking his rod and basket. And tears, or something like them, were dripping down Jake's face; and Silver's voice was queer and wobbly—it was never like that!

Then Dick saw Silver look angrily at Jake, and Jake look angrily at Silver, and at the same moment each man tried to raise him in his arms.

It was Silver who finally lifted him to Jake's shoulder.

"Whatever else we quarrel about," he whispered gruffly, "we'll not squabble over the boy. He is fagged out. Carry him gently and perhaps he may sleep."

So down the trail they went, preceded by Silver, Raoul, and the red-shirted axemen of Peter's gang, all with blazing torches. But tired as Dick was, he could not sleep. The woods were alive with lights that danced to and fro like huge fireflies in the blackness. It was all weird and unreal, and his head ached.

"Are they all hunting for me?" he asked Jake faintly.

"Yes, Dick. Eagle, Sherwood, and the McGregor gangs, they're all out. The boss couldn't stop 'em," answered Jake.

The boy was silent for a while.

"What time is it?" he queried at last. "How long have they been hunting?"

"It's close onto one o'clock now," Jake replied. "We began scourin' the woods about seven."

"So you have all been tramping most of the night! And the men so tired when they knock off work! Oh, Jake!"

"You're worth it, lad. Thank heaven, Raoul could give us some idea where you went," was all Jake said.

Even Mr. Houston, who, with pale face and torn clothing, overtook the party on the down trail, had no word of reproach for Dick, and none was needed. The exhausted, scarred searching parties that came straggling back to McGregor were rebuke enough.

"You won't see me venturing off by myself again, Uncle Alf, or getting away from the trail, either. I am sorry, sir."

"Just put into use every lesson you learn, Dick, and I'll forgive you," was Mr. Houston's terse reply.

CHAPTER V

DICK PLAYS A JOKE

he blow that Dick received by walking off the cliff near the Eagle trail proved not at all serious even though, at the time, it had deprived him of consciousness. In a few days he was himself again and as keenly interested in camp life as ever.

And what a busy life it was! Its variety was never ending. He went on more trouting expeditions with the men; went catching eels one afternoon toward sunset; helped in the laying of logging roads; brought wood and water for the camp; repaired canoes; and tramped from trail to trail as the men finished marking the trees in one lot and changed to another.

With Jake he examined the young growth which they were working to protect, and learned that when trees stood too far apart their trunks grew short and thick and that they put out so many branches that the lumber was full of knots. On the other hand, Jake said that if the trees were left to grow too near together they would be small in diameter, and direct their strength into shooting up for light. Their value as timber would be low because so few boards could be cut from them. Jake and Silver therefore ordered groups of seedlings thinned so they should in future get the right amount of space and light to grow into trees which should yield wide, clear lumber.

Dick was surprised, as he more closely studied the forest, to see how many oaks, chestnuts, and walnuts were scattered among the evergreens.

"I wonder, Jake," he asked one day," how the nut trees happened to be growing here among so many pines and spruces."

"Why, lad, that's the work mostly of squirrels and birds. They pick up the nuts somewhere and carry them from place to place, often dropping them as they go. Of course the nuts take root. Sometimes, too, a hard wind blows them from the trees and scatters them so that they roll away and sprout at long distances from where they grew in the first place. Such trees can start from stumps, too. The pines and other conifers, or cone-bearing trees, are sown by the wind whirling their little winged seeds, which are inside the cones, all about. When a forest is all of one kind of tree we call it a pure forest," continued Jake. " Now and then you find natural pure forests; but generally they have to be planted, and then watched carefully that other kinds of trees may be uprooted and kept out."

"And are all the different sorts of trees good for lumber?" asked Dick.

"Oh, not all of them. Some are more valuable for other things. Poplars, for instance, when ground into wood pulp make excellent paper. Oaks give us not only some of the most solid timber, but their bark is powdered fine and put into the water in which leather is soaked, or tanned. This, as you know, makes the leather tough and strong. There are white oaks, black oaks, red oaks, and, in the South, live oaks. Sometimes dye is made from the bark of the red oak. The black oak is the largest and its bark is most used for tanning because it is cheapest, and also contains the greatest amount of tannin. The red oak has the largest acorns, but its wood is the poorest, and is used a great deal for barrel staves and such things. Walnut trees are more rare and therefore valuable; their wood keeps sound a long time, and furniture makers use it."

"And what about maples?" asked Dick, as Jake stopped for breath.

"Oh, there are lots of kinds of maples, but we get only the white maple, the red maple, and the sugar maple. You'll know the white because its leaves are very green on top and white underneath. It grows larger than any of the other maples, but its wood is so soft and light that it is not much use. The red, or flowering maple, is harder and is grained with fine waving lines that make folks call it the curled maple. A great deal of it is made into furniture. It turns red the minute the first frost comes. The sugar maple is as good for its sap as for its wood, for although all maples give some sap, the sugar maple gives the most. Some of this wood is spotted and is therefore called bird's-eye maple. It is one of the highest-priced woods we have. Did you ever think, Dick, how things seem to even up in the world? Now the sugar maple won't grow in the South. I suppose the Lord gave the Southerners sugar-cane instead. But it's a funny thing, isn't it?"

Dick nodded.

"And then there are birch trees," he mused, reflectively.

"My land, yes—heaps of kinds of 'em! Six or seven, I reckon. First, there's the canoe or white birch—you know all about that, for you've peeled the bark of it often enough. Besides the white birch, there is the gray birch, red birch, yellow birch, and black birch, to my certain knowledge. The yellow is the finest tree of them all, very tall and straight. But the black has the best wood. We get beeches, too, here in Canada, and they are strong and tough—red beech, and white."

"Don't forget chestnuts," laughed Dick, as Jake prepared to go.

"See here, what do you think I am?" gasped Jake. "A walking dictionary, or something? Yes, there are chestnuts that crackle when you burn them; that's because the wood is full of little air-holes, and when the air in them gets hot they burst with a snap. Chestnut trees are queer, too. All their sap circulates in their bark instead of in the wood. It's the same with willows. Sometimes you'll see them growing long after all the inside has rotted away. Chestnut wood is light, soft and not strong and is so filled with little fine holes that there are many things it isn't good for. But you can use it for rails, or for inside doors, or barrels to put dry stuff in; but you couldn't put vinegar in barrels like that."

"You haven't said a word about the evergreens yet," grinned Dick.

"Goodness! Won't you let me breathe, with your catechism? I'm not a talking machine, though you may think I am!"

"I'll bet you don't know anything about the evergreens," Dick chuckled.

"Now see here, you young rascal, I can't sit here on a stump all day giving you the history of every tree in this forest. You think over what I've told you already and if, by to-night, I find you remember any of it I'll not only tell you the rest, but I'll take you off alone with me to-morrow if your uncle is willing, and give you the time of your life."

"Where will you take me, Jake?" demanded Dick eagerly.

"That's my secret," returned Jake, rising.

He gave a hitch to the trousers inside his leather belt, yawned, stretched his great arms, and strolled off to rejoin the men.

Dick, understanding that Jake could not now be prevailed upon to tell anything more that day, tramped back to McGregor Camp where he found Silver, who had just returned from superintending the laying of a new corduroy across a marsh up toward Sherwood.

"Silver," he called. "Please come here. I want you to help me play a joke."

"What is it?" questioned the Frenchman, good-naturedly.

"It's on—Jake," Dick returned a bit timidly. "You see," he hurried on, "he has been giving me a lesson about the trees and already I've forgotten some of it. You must help me out, for if I can't repeat what he told me to-night, he won't take me on some jolly lark he's planned for to-morrow."

Silver grunted.

"You will help me, won't you, Silver?"

"Probably it's all a bluff," Silver answered slowly, eying Dick through half-closed lids. "Like as not he expects you to forget it so he won't have to take you. He was pretty safe in promising."

A shade of disappointment passed over the boy's face.

"I never thought of that. Maybe he did know I'd forget."

"You Sit Here While I Clean My Rifle"

Silver saw the shadow.

"But whether he did or not, we'll spring a surprise on him."

The idea pleased Silver.

"You sit here while I clean my rifle, and while I'm working you tell me all you know about trees, and I'll tell you all I know. Between us we ought to make Jake open his eyes. If he was planning to take you on some jaunt he'll find you ready to go, and if he was fooling and hadn't any plan, why, he'll have to make one, quick."

So through the afternoon Dick recited over and over all that he could remember about chestnuts, oaks, walnuts, maples, and beeches, and he was not a little surprised to discover how much he could recall. This information Silver supplemented with facts he had gathered in his twenty years of work in the forest. By nightfall Dick had his story prepared for Jake.

It was not until after supper that he found the big woodsman alone, drying out his moccasins at one of the campfires.

Dick dropped softly down beside him on the pine needles.

"Hello, youngster!" Jake remarked, going on with his task.

"I've got something to tell you," said Dick.

"Fire ahead, I'm listening. What is it?"

Then with eyes upon Jake's astonished countenance, Dick began. He recited the list of trees as if he were giving an oration, checking each tree off on his fingers when he had told all that he could about it.

Jake did not offer a word.

When the last tree had been crossed from Dick's imaginary list he waited, looking anxiously at Jake.

The forester was puzzled.

"See here," he said, "you have got some stuff there that I never told you in the world. Your uncle's been coaching you."

"No!"

"Well, somebody has. You're putting up a joke on me."

Dick laughed.

"You can't say I have not remembered what you told me," he replied, enjoying Jake's chagrin.

"Remembered! I should say you had. You've added a few points for me, too. I see there is no escape for me! It's up to me now to take you off tomorrow, just as I promised."

Jake scowled, but no one could help seeing the merriment in his eyes.

"Come now," he continued, "own up! Who was it set you going like a phonograph?"

Dick became sober.

"It was—was Silver," he faltered.

Jake was silent.

"Well, laddie," he said finally, "Silver and I have not been the best of friends for a long time; but he's good to you, and that's a big thing in his favor."

"That's just what he said the other day about you, Jake," whispered Dick.

At that moment round the corner of the cabin came Silver himself.

He would instantly have gone back, but Dick called to him eagerly:

"He's going to take me tomorrow, Silver! He really is—no bluff."

The boy's enthusiasm swept all before it.

Jake glanced up at Silver. Then suddenly, for the first time in years, the two men exchanged a smile.

CHAPTER VI

THE DAY WITH JAKE

HE next morning at dawn Dick was promptly astir and, bringing his rods and fish basket, as he had been told to do, met Jake at the cookhouse. Smoke rising from the chimney in a spiral of pale blue showed them that Lutz and Raoul were also awake. After a hearty breakfast the two fishermen packed up the luncheon which kind old Lutz had ready for them, and started off up the Sherwood trail. Halfway to the ridge, they turned off the path through a narrow, fern-bordered ribbon way which went winding off through the trees.

"I never knew there was a trail here," cried Dick. "Where are we going, Jake?"

"It's a trail that isn't used much now, though time was when it was traveled a heap. It goes to Loon Lake—about the most forsaken spot you ever were in, I reckon," responded Jake. "This lake used to be stocked with landlocked salmon once upon a time, and there are still many of them there if anyone ever had the leisure to go and pull them out."

"Oh, Jake! I never caught a landlocked in all my life! How big are they? Are they anything like trout? Do they jump and run the same way?"

"You'll see for yourself, youngster. It's a good seven miles over there yet; and as the lake lies so far out of the way, the men seldom meddle with it. It has not been fished this spring so we'll have all the chance there is to get whatever fish are there. We ought to have pretty good luck."

"Oh, it will be splendid!" Dick exclaimed.

As in the early morning light they traveled the unbroken stillness, the woods seemed never to have been so beautiful. Every fern was drenched with dew, while among the mosses, set in a million glistening drops, glowed clusters of scarlet bunch berries. The air was heavy with moist forest odors, and the music of the great whispering treetops.

"Isn't this a good time to finish up the evergreen lesson?" suggested Dick, mischievously.

"I believe it is," smiled Jake. "There will be just about time to do it."

He was thoughtful a moment, then began:

"Perhaps you don't know that there are lots of kinds of evergreens—pines, spruces, firs, hemlocks, larches, and cedars. The pines have long leaves which are not really like leaves at all, but are much more like bits of smooth wire, growing in bunches. Now the leaves of the spruce are like wire too, only they are short, and arranged like the teeth of a comb along both sides of the branches. Pines and spruces are more used than any other trees in these forests. There are several kinds of pine: white pine, yellow pine, red pine, and gray pine. The white pine is most common, and at the same time most valuable. It grows very high, and its trunk is so straight and tall that it makes the finest masts in the world. You will find its cones full of gum, and they burn wonderfully when dried, because of this gum, or resin. I will tell you about resin by and by. Together with the yellow pine, the wood is used a great deal for building. The yellow, or pitch pine, makes the hottest kind of a fire because its wood is full of resin, from which, you know, turpentine can be made. But generally folks get their tar and turpentine from other trees where the wood is not worth so much—often from the Georgia pitch pine."

"How do they make turpentine, Jake?" questioned Dick.

"They bore for it, as they do for maple sap. From spring to fall it runs, and is about the thickness of molasses, getting thicker and stickier after it stands a while. But you can't keep drawing the sap from a tree more than five or six seasons, for then it won't run. After the turpentine is distilled it leaves an amber gum, thick and hard, called resin."

"Yes, they use that on violin strings," put in Dick. "And turpentine goes into paint."

"And into soap, too," Jake added.

"How do they make tar?"

"Well, I can't tell you all about that, but I do know that it comes from burning the stacked-up limbs, and dead trunks of pine trees. As these smolder, the tar runs into ditches, or somewhere, and is ladled into casks. Of course, you know that sailors use it to paint over the bottom of boats, so as to keep out the water; and they cover boards and ropes with it too, to keep them from rotting."

"And red pine?" Dick asked.

"The red pine is sometimes called the Norway pine. We

get that in these woods, too. Although its wood has not as beautiful grain as the yellow pine, it is hard and durable, and its bark is good for tanning."

As Jake talked he trotted on down the narrow trail while Dick, panting to keep pace with his long, even strides, puffed after him.

"And what about—the—gray—pine?" he managed to gasp.

"'Tain't much of a tree. It grows small. They call it the gray pine because of its gray cones. The wood is used most for making charcoal, and for the frames of canoes."

For a moment he stopped speaking and laughed heartily at two tiny red squirrels that chased each other across the path.

"Now for spruces," he said. "There are three kinds: black, white, and red. Most of Dalton and Company's timber here is red spruce, and it is very hard to tell from the black—that dark, spooky tree ahead, with the small cones hanging down. See? Black spruce grows up in a point, like a pyramid, and because its wood is soft, weak, and lightweight, much of it is made into wood pulp for paper."

"Is there turpentine in it?"

"None to speak of," Jake replied. "Now, white spruce we do not get much here. It is not nearly so common, anyway. Its leaves are pale green and further apart than the black spruce leaves are, and they do not smell as good as other evergreens. The roots are the best part of it, I think, for they are tough as rope and often, when covering a canoe, I have pulled their fibers apart and sewed the birch bark with the thread."

Dick smiled up at the big lumberman.

"How did you know all these things, Jake?" he asked, admiringly.

"Oh, by keeping my eyes open. You can't be penned up in the woods without finding out about the things round you. When you get stuck for something you want—as you pretty often do—why you have just got to flax round and use what you have. It doesn't hurt you a mite not to be able to get strong thread, and to have to shred up spruce roots instead. City folks have things too convenient. They can always get exactly what they want, so they don't have to go ahead and use their brains to make something else do."

"I believe you're right, Jake," returned Dick, soberly.

They walked on in silence for a time.

Then Jake observed:

"You will find hemlock the slowest growing evergreen there is, and you can tell it by its little sharp cones. And if you want to remember something else about hemlock just try once to split its wood, and split it straight. You can't do it to save your life. Now chestnut splits into fine rails, but you never could use hemlock for rails. But its bark is good for tanning. It gives the leather a dark red color when used alone, and when they do not want the leather such a deep color, they mix it with oak bark."

"What's this?"

Dick caught a shiny fragrant evergreen twig in his hand and held it up to Jake.

"That is fir balsam. Resin gathers in sort of blisters on its trunk and branches. Crush it in your hand and see how sweet it smells. We cut it, you know, to sleep on here in camp not only because it smells good, but because its branches are not so stiff as other evergreens. The tree is much like the silver fir, but its wood is so coarse and light that it makes cheap lumber. Now larches, which we find now and then in these forests, have just the opposite kind of timber. It is large and strong, but is too heavy for many things for which it might otherwise be used. It is big enough and strong enough for masts, but it weighs too much. So they use it for ship timber, where heavy wood is needed."

"What do they use cedars for?" asked Dick.

"Red cedar is made into lead pencils. It has a kind of spicy smell and often, too, they make it into chests, and line closets with it. Folks say it keeps out moths. We have not many cedars here, but you can tell them by their rusty green, irregular branches; and their dull blue berries, which grow upon them instead of cones. I reckon that is all I can tell you about evergreens. Now you set about using your own eyes and see if you can't find out something to tell me. There is no reason why you shouldn't. It isn't likely I have found out all there is to know. If you see anything queer about a tree come and tell me, and maybe together we can learn something more."

"There are lots of books on trees," said Dick, eagerly. "When I go home, Jake, I will send you the best one I can find."

"Land alive, laddie, I couldn't read it if you did."

The big fellow flushed, but smiled.

"I went into the woods with my father when I was five years old, and never went to school," he added.

"Well, all I can say, then," Dick replied, slowly, "is that I am ashamed I do not know more—with the chance I've had. But you mustn't feel, Jake, that you have not had quite as many lessons and more, too, than I have." He touched the sleeve of the forester. "The only difference is that you have read yours out of trees, and leaves, and lumber, while I got mine from books. So far, yours are three times as much use as mine."

Jake smiled kindly at the boy over his shoulder, and the two stopped suddenly for, just as the sun was gilding the top of Blue Mountain, they emerged from the trail into a clearing.

A more desolate spot it would be difficult to find! Long ago the entire district had been burned over so thoroughly that now, against a background of ebony, bare silvered tree trunks, bleached by the weather, stood like ghosts. Loon Lake lay in the heart of this charred setting. Nowhere was there a sign of life until, into the stillness, there arose the wail of a loon—a sound so unearthly in the solitude, that both fisher-men started.

"Not a very sociable spot, eh?" questioned Jake. "Well, at least, that loon is glad we've come."

Dick laughed.

"I don't wonder the men let this place alone," he said.

"We are not going to let it alone. It is high time somebody came up here and stirred things up a little."

Starting off toward a rough shelter, Jake dragged out a birch canoe which he and Dick carried to the water's edge and slipped into the lake. Afterward they loaded in fishing-tackle and paddles and were off. A package of lunch, to be cooked later over a fire, they left in the shelter.

"Fix up your rod with a stiff tip, Dick," said Jake, "and I'll paddle while you troll. You'll want that silver spoon hook that turns round in the water, and a couple of scarlet flies."

"I don't want you to do all the work," objected Dick. "I'll fish for a while, and then I will paddle and you must try it."

"Well perhaps I'll have a hand by and by. We'll see what luck you have."

Dick's reel whirred as he played out his line. Then noiselessly they shot off.

They were part way across the lake when, without warning, Dick's rod was almost wrenched from a careless grip.

A fish had struck!

"Play him, lad! Play him! Keep him off from the boat, for he will make a rush underneath. Hold him out! Hold him out! Let him run until he's tired and ready to give up the fight. Now reel in slowly. Steal up on him. Carefully! Now look out. He'll jump out of water in a second. What did I tell you! Now reel in. Land him on this side. I'm all ready with the net."

Dick had not said a word, but had followed Jake's directions minutely—his eyes fastened upon his line. He scarcely breathed.

Slowly he brought the fish nearer and when close to the canoe, raised the rod.

Instantly Jake slipped the net beneath, and there in the canoe lay Dick's first landlock!

Then the boy let himself go.

"Oh, he's a beauty, Jake! Look at him! Four or five pounds, don't you think? My, but that was sport."

"Now hit him on the head," Jake commanded. "It makes me sick to see any critter suffer. They're kind of friends of mine. You can just as well kill a fish as to let it lie out of water and gasp. Remember that! Some folks say animals don't mind, but you'll never make me believe that. There's two things I never do: one is to let any critter suffer; and the other is to kill any critter that I do not mean to use, unless it is doing real harm."

"I'll try and remember those two things, too, Jake," Dick said, once more letting out his line.

It was wonderful fishing that morning. One after another the large salmon were hauled into the canoe.

Jake had his turn too, for Dick insisted upon taking the paddle when they recrossed the lake.

When the sun was well up, it began to be hot, and they landed and took a swim. Afterward, kindling a fire, they prepared to cook a meal upon a spider over the coals, for they had breakfasted before sunrise and were very hungry. Dick went up to the lean-to for the bundle of bacon, potatoes and coffee, while Jake heaped up the fire.

But search as he might, Dick failed to find the package Lutz had given them.

"Hello, Jake!" he called. "Where on earth did you put the food? It isn't here, or else I've suddenly gone blind."

Jake strode up to the shelter, but before he was half-way there he stooped to examine a crushed birch seedling lying across his path. Then he sprang up, alert. He dashed up to the hut; looked about carefully; noted the bruised ferns near the doorway, and the trail of mud leading off into the brush.

"What is it?" asked Dick anxiously.

"We'll get no meal today. It's gone! Bruin has taken it. I was an idiot to come up here without a rifle, or we might track him. He has gone up Blue Mountain, and he has not been gone long, for the mud stains are not yet dry. But it is useless for us to try it without a gun. We'll just have to let him go."

Dick was all excitement.

"A real bear! Think of it, Jake! Oh, I'd give anything for a shot at him!"

"Put Out The Fire"

"Well, Dickie," exclaimed Jake with relief, "all I can say is I'm almighty glad you didn't find him waiting for you in the shelter when you went for the food. I guess your uncle won't be so ready to trust you with me again, when he hears I was such a careless guide as to come out unarmed. It is never safe in these woods. I've got my lesson this time. If anything had happened to you—"

He broke off abruptly.

"Now we'll stow away the canoe and put out the fire," he went on, after a little pause. "Remember always, when in the woods, Dick, to be sure before you leave a fire that not a spark of it remains. Some of the worst fires have come from careless campers leaving a fire which was not fully out. That's what happened here, and look at the place! Not only did a few smoldering pine-needles destroy this whole section, but they endangered acres of other timber."

"Tell me about it," begged Dick, as they heaped earth upon their own tiny bed of coals, packed up their rods, and started back toward McGregor.

"'Twas in a dry season. Dalton and Company forbade any men to light fires except at the main camps where they had water near at hand, and plenty of men to watch them. Well," Jake hesitated, "somebody disobeyed and lit a fire up here. He did not put it entirely out before he left, though why he didn't, knowing all he knew of the woods, I cannot see!"

Dick became breathless. Before he put the question that rose to his lips he had answered it.

"It was Silver!" he remarked, half aloud.

"Maybe it was, and then again maybe it wasn't," hurried on Jake, uncomfortably. "Anyhow, that fire cost Dalton and

Company thousands of dollars, and the man would have lost his job but for his fine record with the firm, and the pleading of his friends. Your uncle had to work like a steer to make them keep him."

"Who reported him to Mr. Dalton?"

"I did. I was foreman at the time, and I had to do it in the interest of the company. But before I took the case to Dalton I made as careful an investigation as ever a man could. I gave every lumber-jack in the camp a chance to confess it, if he had had any hand in the fire. Silver was the one who came forward and he took every scrap of the blame. He said he went up there alone—a mighty queer thing for him to do, too—and he built the fire; he cooked some trout; and he put the fire out, or thought he did. That was all he'd say. He wouldn't offer one excuse or explanation. So, you see, there was nothing for me but to do my duty, and inform the firm. That was the beginning of my trouble with Silver. He has been down on me ever since."

"It doesn't seem like him to do such a crazy thing as leave a smoldering fire," mused Dick.

"No more it does, and yet he is a reckless fellow sometimes—more reckless about himself than anything else. He does not give a fig for his life. You should see him on the drive. He runs those logs as if there was no such thing as being drowned; and any time there is a real giant's chore to be done, he is always the man who offers. He says he has no one depending on him as the others with families have. Anyway, we had a fight to stop this fire, I can tell you!"

"How did you do it?" questioned Dick, diverted for the instant from Silver.

"Well, unfortunately the fire had gained quite a headway; but there happened to be only a thin covering of dry stuff on the ground in from the lake, so it could not burn very fast. If we had had a deep layer of pine-needles and such, it would have been another matter. But a fire like this one, though it killed the trees round the lake, was not hot enough to do more than injure the bark of the others off in the woods, and lick up the young growth. What worried us most was that off to the west were stretches of pure pine and spruce where the floor was deep with needles and dried branches. These would burn like tinder if the flames reached them. I tell you it gave the men a lesson in leaving old limbs loose on the ground to dry after cutting, instead of gathering them up as we do now. What we did was to start another fire between those woods and the one burning toward us from the lake."

"What on earth did you do that for?"

"Why, you see the wind was just the way so the fire we made couldn't burn forward into the pines and spruces. It could only burn back and meet the other that was coming. So when the one came sweeping along from the lake it burned up to the place that we had burned over and when it got there, there was nothing for it to burn, and it died down. We put it out after a while, though it smoked for ever so long. But you do not want to try to stop a forest fire that way unless you are sure of the wind, and even then it changes suddenly sometimes and leaves you worse off than if you had let things alone."

"How did you put the fire out?"

"Oh, luckily it did not get into the tree tops—that is the most dangerous kind of a fire—one that burns on the ground and overhead, too. No, this one was just on the ground, and we beat it out with green branches, and heaped sand on it wherever we could. But the wind beating it back was our biggest help."

"Can't a fire ever move with a strong wind against it?"

"Just about never. But nowadays we are better prepared against fires in these woods. We have made a checker-board of this timber and crisscrossed it with broad bands of bare earth where not a spear of anything grows. Unless a fire was burning overhead and was a rager, it would have quite a job to jump those belts of dirt. Of course if it burrowed it might."

"What do you mean by burrowing?" Dick asked.

"Why, sometimes fires get down beneath the surface into peat or something, and smolder there for weeks without a soul knowing they are there. They travel along this way underground and then some day surprise you by bursting out on the surface. It is a mean kind of a fire to fight, for it shows almost no smoke, and you can't place it. You would think rain would put it out, but often it is so far down that the water does not get to it. You have just got to dig a trench deep enough to get clear of everything in the soil that will burn, and when such a fire gets walled round with those trenches it has to stop."

By this time McGregor came into view. The two fishermen, hot and tired from their tramp, were glad enough to drop their catch of landlock at the cook-house door and stop for a moment where the stiff western breeze swept off the lake.

Then Jake seized a quarter of a dried apple pie and was off to join the gang at Eagle, while Dick and Raoul started in cleaning the salmon for supper.

But Dick worked absent-mindedly. He was thinking over the story of the fire at Loon Lake.

"It does not seem like Silver," he kept repeating to himself. "Some day I mean to find out if he really did it."

CHAPTER VII

A WILD GOOSE CHASE
AND HOW IT ENDED

I T was not long before Dick had the wished-for opportunity to talk with Silver, for in a day or two he met the lumberman returning from Sherwood, where he had been superintending the laying of corduroys and roll ways.

"Well, Dick, how goes it?" called Silver.

"Better and better every day," was the boy's reply.

Silver rubbed his hands.

"You've taken to the woods as a duck takes to water," he said. "So it's not such a bad thing to be packed off to a lumber camp, after all?"

"I should say not. It's great!"

"But you haven't seen zero weather in the pines yet, remember," grinned the Canadian. "Wait until it is black as your shoe every morning, and cold as the North Pole! That's the time the men fuss about getting out to work. And winter is on the way. Almost every maple has turned and dropped, and the boys say there were five inches of snow up on Blue Mountain yesterday morning. Now that the law is off, you and I will have to be doing some shooting."

"Oh, Silver! I wish we could. Do you ever get time to go?"

"I reckon I can make time some day. Listen! Do you hear those loons? There must be a score of them. There they are, sure enough. See? A whole procession of them, swimming up toward the Point."

"Let's chase them, Silver. Come ahead! I want dreadfully to shoot a loon. Uncle Alf says it is great sport."

Silver smiled at Dick's eagerness.

"Get your rifle then, and come on. You shoot a loon, and we'll put you down as a true-blue sportsman. You will have plenty of chance to try, too, for there are at least fifteen in sight now."

Silver took a big, battered timepiece from out his hip pocket.

"There is a little over an hour before the horn for dinner. Be off with you now, lively. Bring my rifle too, and I'll be getting the canoe into the water while you're gone."

Dick ran to the gun-rack at the front of the bunk-house where Silver slept, and after securing the woodsman's rifle, snatched his own from the cabin. Meantime Silver awaited him in the canoe, steadying it near shore with the paddle.

Dick slipped into the light craft and they shot out into the lake.

"Now you mustn't make a sound," cautioned Silver. "Loons are canny. Lie low in the bottom of the boat. We'll try to steal up on them. It's easier said than done, though."

Dick crouched obediently in the canoe, loading his rifle

as noiselessly as he could, while Silver sent them through the water with that absolute stillness possible only to one expert in dipping the paddle. They shaped their course toward the dam at the lower end of McGregor, from whence a file of about a dozen loons were now approaching.

All excitement, Dick peeped over the edge of the boat.

The great birds, with snowy breasts and quick-shifting heads, stood up out of the choppy waters of the lake with wonderful distinctness.

"Wait for a close shot," whispered Silver, "for if you miss, it's off they go."

Dick waited, scarcely drawing a breath. He was about to raise himself and fire when suddenly the leader gave a weird laugh and dove beneath the waves, only to be followed by the others.

Disappointed, the boy sat up.

"I didn't make a sound. Now what should take them all off like that?"

"That's the loon of it," laughed Silver softly. "Watch for them to rise. Where do you think they will come up?"

Silently, Dick pointed inshore.

"Just you wait and see. They are contrary as a lot of mules, and are never known to come up where you think they will. That's the fun of chasing them."

"Ha-a-a-a-ah!" called the loon.

"There he is! There he is—the leader!" Dick exclaimed. "Where are the others?"

"Scattered. They'll come up all round us. Lie low, and we'll go after the nearest one."

As Silver deftly turned the canoe and bent his strength

to the paddle, they sped through tiny billows which sent up swirls of spray.

Dick's fingers tightened on his rifle.

"Now try that bird ahead," Silver directed, "the last one of those three."

Rising carefully, Dick spied a single loon drifting unconcernedly across their bows.

Instantly a report echoed from one end of the lake to the other.

He scanned the water eagerly.

"Missed!" announced Silver, as the creature ducked, only to come up with a tantalizing jeer in their wake.

He waited, then tried again.

Once more the loon evaded him.

Again he tried.

The loon ducked for safety.

"He's making fun of me. I can't get him. I had no idea it would be so hard," the boy declared, impatient at his failures. "You try it, Silver, and let me paddle."

"I should like one crack at them," admitted Silver. "Now carefully. Canoes are not made to change seats in, especially in deep water. Slide along to the left. There you are! Now head her inshore."

Dick obeyed.

His stroke was not so firm as Silver's, and the wind was against him; but he managed to keep the nose of the canoe to her course, and make moderate headway.

Three of the loons were now on their left, and Dick hoped to pen them in toward the Point unless they ducked.

He had crept well up on them when, with a bang, Silver's rifle cleft the stillness.

"I've missed, too," the lumberman grinned. "This is a wild goose chase, sure enough. We shall not get one, I'm afraid. They are too wise. The men have been after them so often that it has taught them a thing or two. We ought to have Jake here. He is the best shot in camp."

Dick looked up in surprise.

"Jake is a great shot," he echoed timidly, not knowing just what to reply. "And he is a great fisherman, too. The day we went up to Loon Lake—" He stopped.

"He took you up there, did he?" questioned Silver, drily. "I wondered how that excursion he promised you turned out."

"Yes, that's where we got that big string of landlocks."

"Kind of a bare spot—Loon Lake," Silver observed, eying the boy keenly.

"Yes, it is."

"I reckon," the lumber-jack ventured at last, drawling out his words with studied carelessness, "he told you about the fire there."

"Yes."

Dick was crimson with discomfort.

"Of course. Perfectly natural he should. But somehow I'm sorter sorry you had to know it, Dickie. I'd rather like to have you hold a better opinion of me than that."

"But you did not really set the fire, Silver," Dick answered, quickly. "You never could have done it, even if everybody thinks you did."

A light came into the eyes of the woodsman.

"But I myself told 'em to blame me."

"Maybe, but you didn't do it."

Conviction rose in Dick's heart as he met the glance of the man before him.

"But why should I let them think so, if I didn't do it?" persisted Silver.

"I don't know why. I don't understand it at all. I just know you did not set that fire."

"Well, Dick—if only the rest of them had half your faith!"

"Then you didn't really do it?" queried Dick eagerly.

"I'm not saying that," the forester protested, becoming reserved. "Somebody set that fire, and the blame was fixed on me. I wanted the blame. But remember, Dick, I never told anybody I started the fire. If Jake had thought carefully, afterward, he would have noticed that. He had always been my best friend in camp. For years we had worked together here. I did not mind his reporting me, for I wanted to be the one punished; but I did think he knew me too well to believe I could do such a thing. That's what cut me."

"Silver," Dick said softly, "who did set the Loon Lake fire? You know who it was, and you have some reason for taking the blame. Come, be honest. Who did it?"

But Silver was on his guard.

"There are a score of things, lad, that you don't know; and a score more that you never will. This is one of them. What I've said, you can keep to yourself. Silence isn't a bad thing in this world. The forest teaches that lesson, if it teaches no other. There is a sight more harm comes from talking than from keeping still. But I'll tell you one thing—you're a good lad, Dick!"

Then suddenly finding a lump rising in his throat, the

The Forester Dropped The Paddle

lumberman gave a harsh laugh and, taking up the other paddle which lay in the bottom of the boat, began to help the boy.

In silence they dashed on, Silver's powerful stroke shaking the canoe with every forward leap.

Then suddenly there was a whirr of wings. A triangle of black ducks wheeled up over the trees bordering the Point and, rising high overhead, made across the lake.

The forester dropped the paddle, and his gun was in his hand.

There was a deafening report.

The leader fell.

Again Silver fired.

Another of the birds fluttered headlong to the water.

A third shot brought down nothing, but at the fourth one more duck dropped.

Then the remainder, demoralized, flapped out of sight.

Dick paddled quickly to where the fallen creatures bobbed on the top of the water, and picked them up.

Then the hunters struck out for shore.

"Nothing like starting out for loon and coming home with duck," chuckled Silver, in high spirits.

Grounding the craft on the sandy beach at the Point, the two sprang out and carried the canoe to shelter where they turned it bottom upward.

Afterward, with their rifles and the three ducks, they went up to the camp, where they found Mr. Houston and Jake welcoming two strangers who had just come in over the carry.

"That is the Game Commissioner, Mr. Dearborn; and Mr. Davies, the warden of this district. Fine men, both of them!" explained Silver. "They come in every fall."

"What for?" asked Dick.

"Oh, Mr. Dearborn is a friend of your uncle's, and comes chiefly for a neighborly call. The warden, of course, comes to see that we are keeping the fish and game laws."

As Silver answered, they had neared the group.

Mr. Dearborn turned.

"Why, if here isn't my friend Silver!" he exclaimed. "How are you, Silver? You have been doing damage with your rifle, I see. Well, I am just in time to help eat up some of those black ducks."

He shook Silver's big hand cordially.

"It is jolly to see the old Dalton men again," he added to Mr. Houston. "Who is this boy?"

He motioned to Dick. "I do not seem to recall him."

"That is my nephew, Dick Sherman," Mr. Houston replied. "Dick, this is Mr. Dearborn; and this, Mr. Davies. They have come to see if we are living up to the good laws they have made to protect the fish and game in this region."

"Oh, we do not have to visit Dalton's camps for that," protested Mr. Davies, "because we know before we come there is no more honest, decent set of fellows than Dalton's men."

"Well, I'll tell you frankly, sheriff, the law has been broken up here once this season."

The warden became grave.

Even Silver and Jake looked disturbed.

"Yes," went on Mr. Houston, "a buck was killed out of season, and although I did not actually hold the gun, I urged on the offender. But I am ready to pay the fine—it was worth it to see Dick, here, make his first shot. I never did such a thing before in my life, and suppose I never shall again. But I was afraid the boy might have to wait years for another such chance, so I let him go ahead. At the time, he did not know anything about the laws. We have explained all that to him since, for he wants to be a clean-handed sportsman, like the rest of the lumber-jacks."

"Indeed I do," broke in Dick.

"So we'll pay our fine," went on Mr. Houston, pulling out a roll of bills and handing some of them to the warden, "and we promise never to do so again. Yesterday I squared things with the deer family by letting a fine pair of antlers go free to make up for the pair we took. That is our only out-of-season crime, I think. Isn't it, Jake?"

"Yes, sir. Not another in camp. We have lived up to every game law, so far as I know. The men take a tremendous pride in being good forest citizens. They seem to feel that up here they are out of the path of most of the laws of the country, so the least they can do is to keep whatever laws there are; and keep them, even if there isn't a policeman at the turn of every trail. If a trout looks undersized the boys measure him, and if he does not reach from the butt of the rod to the top of the reel—seat—back he goes. And they are careful not to handle the trout with dry hands, for they all understand that will cause fungus to form and the fish will die wretchedly. What's more, Mr. Davies, I do not think we take more than our share of beast, fish, or fowl."

"I am sure you do not. How I wish you fellows could go out and help preach the gospel of clean, honest sportsmanship!" sighed Mr. Davies.

"Well, after all," concluded Jake, "isn't it for everybody's advantage to be decent about it? It is only protecting what lives in the woods as carefully as we are trying here to protect what grows in the woods. We all want to see that things are not wasted, or treated so heedlessly that by and by we won't have any more trees or animals."

"Very true, my man. I wish every hunter and woodsman realized this," put in Mr. Dearborn. "But I suppose if they did there would be no more wardens, and then what would become of our friend Davies?"

He broke into a big, ringing laugh in which everybody joined.

It was just as a few quiet seconds were succeeding this jest that there was a crackling of brush, and up from the edge of the lake a deer bounded into the further end of the clearing.

Silver, who was about to enter the cook-house, at once sighted the creature and raised his rifle. But no sooner had he done so than round the corner of the cabin, directly within range of the ball, came Raoul.

Instantly Jake sprang forward and crouching beneath the line of fire, grasped the lad round the knees, hurling him to the earth just as the ball whistled over his head.

Meantime Silver, white with horror, had staggered back against the cabin where the gun, slipping from his nerveless fingers, crashed to the ground and he fell beside it, covering his face with his hands.

Mr. Houston ran to his side.

The man was shaking from head to foot.

"He is not hurt, Silver. Raoul is safe. Be calm, my man. The boy is not hurt."

With firm grip Mr. Houston dragged the hands of the shrinking lumberman from his eyes that he might see Raoul.

Silver looked.

Then unnerved by the reaction, he broke into sobs.

"The boy—my brother—dearer to me than anyone in the world! The only kin I have. If I had killed him—!"

"But he is safe," repeated Mr. Houston gently, "safe, because Jake saved his life. It was a wonderful thing, to think and act so quickly. If he had not—"

Silver raised his head.

Then getting to his feet he staggered uncertainly to the spot where Jake was raising Raoul, and brushing off the pine-needles that clung to his woolen clothing.

"Jake!"

It was one word—the only word Silver was capable of uttering—but as he spoke it he held out a shaking hand.

The forester strode toward him and took the hand in his big, hearty grasp, but he could not speak.

Silently the two men looked long into each other's eyes.

Then Jake placed his other hand on Silver's shoulder.

"It is all right, old man. Thank heaven, not me! I know how dear the lad is to you. I had a brother once."

A clear voice, the voice of Raoul himself, suddenly broke in upon them.

"I must tell you, Jake; and you, too, Mr. Houston. I cannot bear to have Silver misjudged any longer. It was I who was to blame for the Loon Lake fire."

Silver tried to stop his brother, but the boy refused to listen.

"Yes, it was I! You know how Silver went to Mr. Dalton when my parents died, and begged to bring me into camp. He wanted to have me with him because there was no one else to look out for me. I was only ten then, and Mr. Dalton said he did not care to have a child here. But Silver pleaded, and at last Mr. Dalton said if Silver would answer for me, I might come. I tried to do my best, indeed I did. I did all the little things I could think of for Silver, such as cleaning his rifle; drying his clothes; running his errands. Then a day came when I disobeyed. I went up to Loon Lake—unknown to anyone—caught some trout, and building a fire, cooked them. We had all been warned of the dry season and told not to build fires, but I was sure I could be careful and put mine entirely out. What I did not know was that fires could burrow into the peat, and break out later. That was what my fire did. When the great blaze at Loon Lake came and everyone was wondering how it started, I told Silver about the fire I had built there two days before and so carefully put out."

Raoul waited a moment.

"Then Silver explained to me that it must have been my own fire that had set that dreadful blaze going. He told me that Mr. Dalton would certainly send me out of camp if he knew it, and that if I went, he must go too, for he could not let me live by myself in the town. Moreover he said that he had promised Mr. Dalton to be responsible for what I did, and if I did wrong he must, of course, take the blame. He talked and talked until he convinced me it was the only way. But I have never felt happy or honest about it. I am older now, and I want to go to Mr. Dalton myself, explain it to him, and take my punishment. Then he can clear Silver of blame."

It was Mr. Houston who broke the long silence after Raoul ceased speaking.

"You shall see Mr. Dalton, Raoul. It is only right that you should do so. But I shall send with you a letter telling him that since those days you have grown into one of our most wise and careful woodsmen, and that we have no more useful man at McGregor Camp than you. You have made up for your fearful mistake, and I am sure he need never fear you will make another such. If he still hesitates to trust you, I myself will vouch for your future conduct."

"So will I!" put in Jake.

The next morning when Mr. Dearborn and Mr. Davies went out over the carry Raoul, setting forth for Mr. Dalton's offices at Belleport, went with them. It was three days before he returned. Then he brought with him the full forgiveness of the company. And every woodsman was glad of it.

So closer and closer drew the bonds of friendship between the laborers and those for whom they labored, and peace serene as the forest itself reigned at McGregor Camp.

CHAPTER VIII

THE RING OF THE AXE

ITH the first light snow Dick discovered that, as Mr. Houston had said, the forest had indeed its own people—a population far greater than he had before realized. From every direction tracks in the whiteness told of the silent comings and goings of innumerable creatures. These impressions ranged from the fan-shaped print of the rabbit, and the print like a baby's hand left by the raccoon, to the larger hoof-marks of deer, moose, and black bear. Dick was never tired of examining these traces of his woodland neighbors, and before long could tell one from another almost as quickly as Jake or Silver.

Heavier snows fell.

Then followed the zero weather predicted by Silver when biting winds blew from the lake; branches of bare trees creaked dismally; pines sagged with ice; and you could see your breath—white and frosty—in the wintry air. Morning was inky as midnight; and the sun, setting early behind great bars of gold or copper, shot across the water flaming reflections which mellowed the cabins and tinted the pines half-way to their plumy tips.

Simultaneously with the coming of the snows the camp awakened as from a sleep; and life, which Dick had considered busy enough before, now throbbed with doubled energy. This was the weather they had been waiting for! Roads were broken out and sprinkled so they would freeze into ice which should make smooth the hauling.

From morning until night the blacksmith at McGregor fed his forge tirelessly, welding chains and mending sledge-runners.

The grindstone nearby added its whirr to the din, and sent out showers of sparks as axes took a keener edge.

Big saws were filed ready for work; and the carpenter was constantly fitting axe handles of ash to gleaming blades.

The lumber-jacks themselves, drawing tighter the straps round their waists, moved with new purpose. Their eyes brightened, their voices rang with clearer note.

This wave of activity swept everyone before it, and Dick—thrilled by the onrush—was whirled along with the rest.

It being the outset of the cutting season, Mr. Houston called together the men from the three camps.

"There are certain laws we must all follow," he said, "if we are to carry out the policy of Dalton and Company and put their timber in the finest of condition. One is that every tree marked shall be cut. Now do not leave a tree because it is in an inconvenient place to haul out, and will make you lots of trouble. Get that tree, no matter if it does take time. On the other hand, do not let us find one tree cut which has not been marked. We want no blunderers here!"

Although his words were curt, his tone was kindly, and he smiled.

"Most of you older men," he continued, "know that no stump is to be cut more than six inches higher than the stump is wide. That simply wastes the best part of the lumber. You younger fellows remember that. Then plan your tree to fall in the direction where it will do the least injury to other trees. If, in falling, it bends down saplings or crashes into seedlings, free them as soon as you can, so they will not die; and spare the branches of the larger trees every whit possible. It is no use for us to take all this trouble to protect young trees, and then ruin them when we cut the veterans, is it?"

Mr. Houston looked into the faces before him good-naturedly.

"And just two things more. After you have cut a tree do not leave it where the haulers won't see it. Get it out in plain sight so it won't be left behind. Use no spruce for corduroys, skids, or slides, for it is too good to be wasted that way. If you can't get any other wood, of course you will have to use it; but if you do, you must cut it up afterward, haul it, and send it down with the drive. It is bad enough to have to use such quantities of spruce as we must for camps, dams, and booms, but that is all necessary. On no account use it where it isn't necessary. Does every man here understand?"

There was a shout of assent.

"And, lastly, do not let me find a man here leaving loose branches to dry in these woods. They are fire-breeders! After your branches are lopped off, get them together. They can be collected and burned in the camps; the balsam boughs can be used for fresh bunks; you can repair the carries with some, to prevent washouts. But do not make a fire-trap of this timber by cluttering the ground with such inflammable stuff as branches of dried foliage. If for any good reason you cannot haul off these branches, cut off all twigs projecting on the underside, so the branch can get down close to the soil, and rot there. Now I think that is all. Jake or Silver will advise any of you who do not fully understand these directions. They are to see that the rules are carried out. Do not let them have to send any one of you out over the carry, for Dalton's men are the finest fellows under the shade of the timber, and the company wants to keep every one of them. But I will tell you frankly no man is so valuable to Mr. Dalton that he can allow him to ruin these forests. Good luck to you all!"

Mr. Houston waved a dismissal to the picturesque crowd about him.

"Hurrah for this year's drive!" shouted a big axeman.

"*Hurrah!*" responded the men.

"Hurrah for Dalton and Company!" cried another man.

"*Hurrah!*" roared the lumbermen.

"Hurrah for Mr. Houston, the kindest boss a gang ever had!" yelled a man who shouldered a saw.

"*Hurrah!*"

"Hurrah for Jake—one of the best fellows ever made!" another axeman led the wild "*Hurrah!*" that followed.

"Hurrah for Silver—the other best fellow ever made!" shrieked the tallest Canadian of Peter's gang.

It was given with a will.

Then Silver turned, and in an instant had swept Dick up onto his shoulder.

"Hurrah for Dick Sherman—the little brother of every Dalton lumberman!"

There was a shout that almost made the tree tops tremble.

Blushing, Dick bowed his thanks in the most polite fashion he knew and begged Silver to put him down. Just before he wriggled out of the great arms encircling him he shouted:

"Three cheers for *everybody*!"

The crowd laughed, but following the lead of the red stocking cap Dick waved in his hand, gave the cheers lustily.

Then the groups separated across the frozen roadway.

Dick followed the sledges and men going toward the Eagle lot, for he was anxious to see every part of this wonderful process for which they had been since spring preparing.

Some of the rivermen who had been out with an unusually long drive, and who had but recently returned from the Dalton lumber yards at Belleport, now fell into line with the rest.

It was a sharp day, but the sun filtered through the trees in brilliant rifts, setting a glitter every corner of the forest.

As they went along, one of the men began to sing, and in another moment a chorus of voices took up the song—a strange, rhythmic harmony of the river.

Then, in the heart of the pines, the sledges stopped.

Sawers came forward; axemen stood waiting directions; heaps of chains clanged onto the ice. The foreman stationed his men at the further boundary of the lot so that they might move forward and not miss one marked tree.

Several sturdy fellows with saws and axes were directed toward a veteran pine near the line.

Dick followed them. They had been employed by Dalton and Company for years and therefore needed few orders.

First they walked about the tree, estimating the distance the huge trunk would reach when stretched on the ground, and deciding in which direction its fall would do the least damage.

"We mustn't let her crash into those oaks," said the tallest man.

"Or onto those pine saplings," declared another.

"Why not aim her this way? She will come down into that gap at the left and only brush those chestnuts way over there with her tip."

"All right. Sail ahead!"

One of Peter's gang then took up his axe and chopped a gash in the trunk of the tree on the side where they wished it to fall. This cut was about as far from the ground as the tree was wide.

Then two men took up their long, double-handled saw, one at either end.

With the first gnawing of the sharp blade into the timber, a quiver passed through Dick. He had come so to love these giant pines that it seemed as if he must cry out to the men to stop. But afterward he remembered how his uncle had told him that trees ripened to be of use to man; and that if they were not cut when they had reached their growth, their strength would go and they would begin to decay. And Dick actually smiled at his own foolishness when he recalled that it was Uncle Alf himself who had marked that very tree for cutting. So he waited.

The saw went monotonously on.

Presently the sawers stopped to slip a steel wedge into the cut.

"What's that for?" asked Dick.

"That keeps the weight of the tree from coming down on the saw, which spoils it. Besides, it saws more freely."

Then they went sawing on as before.

After a little they stopped again.

This time they put in a larger wedge and tipped some kerosene on the blade of the saw to make it move easier. They repeated this operation from time to time.

Then a shiver ran through the great tree.

The men motioned Dick close beside them.

They took up their axes.

A few strokes, and another tremor shook the trunk.

It trembled, swayed, tottered.

Then with a cry of "Tim-*ber!*" from the woodsmen, the mighty pine crashed to the earth.

It had fallen exactly where the men had planned to have it, which seemed a very wonderful thing to Dick.

They ran quickly to its tip, releasing and straightening up the young trees pinioned beneath. Afterward they began to clear the trunk of branches, being careful not to gash it. These branches they dragged out and heaped near by. Then they examined the trunk, marking it off into lengths so to avoid all knots, forks, and rotten spots. These lengths differed according to the space between the blemishes they wished to avoid. Some of them were eighteen feet long, some sixteen feet, some fourteen, and some twelve.

When the entire trunk had been sawed into logs, the logs were dragged on sledges over ice roads and skidded, or piled. These piles were called skidways or rollways. Sometimes if the logs could not be reached by the sledge, a chain was fastened round them and horses or a dummy engine hauled them out.

Those who skidded the logs used cant-hooks to swing them into place.

Dick discovered that this was both hard and dangerous work because the logs rolled down very easily and were liable to fall on the men.

As he stood watching the cant-hook men, another man, called the scaler, came and measured the diameter of the logs in the skidway; reckoned up the number of board feet in the pile marked it with colored crayon to show it had been measured; put a record of it in his book; and stamped each log with the "*D. C.*" of the Dalton Company.

This imprint greatly interested Dick.

"Why do you put that mark on every log?" he questioned.

"Why, you see, sonny, a great many logs beside ours go down the Elk River in drives. What would happen if they were not marked?"

"Oh, I see," said Dick. "Of course they would all get mixed up and none of you would know which were his."

"Beside that," the scaler explained, "no one can steal the logs of another company. Each set of rivermen can weed out their own without having any squabbles about it."

"I see," answered Dick. "I never thought of that."

The boy lifted up the sledge-hammer with which the scaler was marking the logs and examined it. In its face were cut the letters "*D. C.*"

Harper, the scaler, let Dick try it and he hacked away on a bit of fresh timber, but found he could not make a clear imprint.

"I can't do it the way you do, Harper," laughed Dick.

"It takes both strength and practice, Dick. I wouldn't try it any more for I am afraid you will get hurt."

So Dick gave over the hammer to Harper with the inward resolve that some day he would come back to the Dalton timber and swing that fascinating tool as jauntily as Harper himself.

CHAPTER IX

CHRISTMAS IN THE WOODS

HROUGHOUT the winter Dick never flinched from the cold, and was out as early as any lumberjack.

Sometimes he spent an entire day with Harper watching the blue scrawls the scaler put on the logs, as he kept tally of the board feet in the rollways.

Other mornings he followed Jake and the foreman up the side of Blue Mountain, where the Sherwood crews, or gangs, were getting out timber. The sort of work done there was new to the boy, for steel cables were stretched across the ravine, and the logs came dangling through the air by means of pulleys.

"This method saves hauling them down the mountain-side and up out of the rough valley, you see," explained Jake. "Horses never could do it and even if we hauled them by steam with a donkey engine, they would bump along the ground and injure other trees. Besides, it would take about five times as long."

So the cables were fastened to some mast-like pine and the chains holding the logs were caught between huge iron tongs and thus traveled safely across the gorge.

The process was very interesting to Dick.

"All the logs from Sherwood," continued Jake, "have to be brought across McGregor Lake to the head waters of the McGregor River; so as fast as the crews get them out, they are made into booms. These booms are built by chaining logs end to end round a large group of loose logs. When the last two logs are joined so the boom is completed we lumber-jacks call it 'marrying the boom.'"

"Where do they build the booms?" questioned Dick.

"Right on the ice," Jake answered. "They are left there until the lake breaks up so they can be warped across to the head of the river."

"Why do you call it warping, and how do they do it?" Dick shot out the two questions at once.

"They have a raft called the head-works, with a big spool or capstan on it. This capstan has eight bars sticking out from the top so they can be used to turn the spool. An anchor is boated out ahead and dropped, and then the booming-crew turn the capstan and spool up the long cable attached to this anchor. Then the raft is left to sail along under its own head-way and the crew boat out the anchor again while two of the men feed the warp off the spool. They keep doing this until the boom gets across the lake. It is rather a slow way but, as the distance is not great and the Sherwood logs are the only ones to go down in this fashion, Dalton and Company have not felt it necessary to buy a launch or tug for the purpose. I expect they will get round to that later."

"How do the Eagle logs get down to the Elk?" asked Dick.

"The Eagle logs are sluiced down a branch of Raven Brook," Jake replied. "It isn't much of a stream, so we have built a series of splash-dams, or sluices, with which we hold the current back until we have high water. Then we lift the gate, sending the logs far down on the flood. This water we hold back in turn by a dam further along stream, and we again let the brook rise and sluice the logs still further on. In this way we carry them down to Raven Brook itself, and from there we have water enough to bring them into the McGregor River, where they join the main drive, and go on to the Elk."

"And the McGregor logs I know about," laughed Dick.

"I reckon you ought to. If you don't, it is your own fault. You have ridden across the ice on the sledges enough times when the logs were hauled from the Point to the head of the river, and piled at the water's edge. Some of those piles will be thirty feet high by the time we finish getting out our lumber. They will stand there until the water rises this spring and floats the lower part of the pile. Then the top will cascade into the stream like a little Niagara, and they will go shooting down river. Now and then, when the logs do not slide in as they should, we have to take axes and cant-hooks and start them. We call this breaking them out. It is dangerous work if they happen to roll down suddenly."

"And the McGregor River flows into the Elk?" Dick questioned.

"Yes. Our drive is known as the Elk River Drive because every drive takes its name from the stream it comes down. We strike the Elk below Sparville. There the Eagle crews meet us with their timber, and the whole drive then goes down the Elk to Belleport, where the Dalton mills are."

Dick rubbed his hands.

"I do hope," he exclaimed, "Uncle Alf will let me go out with the drive this spring."

"It's no easy trip, Dick—I'll tell you that. But you can ask him," was Jake's response.

So when Dick joined his uncle in their cabin that night the first thing he said was:

"Uncle Alf, you will let me go down river this spring when the drive goes out, won't you?"

"You may start, Dick," Mr. Houston answered. "I don't wonder you are anxious to see your trees reach their resting place in the mill. But you forget it will be three months or more before they get down the Elk to Belleport. Your mother wants you at home by the first of the summer.

"Home!" exclaimed Dick, vaguely.

"Yes, my boy. Surely you have not forgotten you have a home."

"No indeed, Uncle Alf. But it seems as if I never could leave McGregor and Jake, Silver, Lutz, Harper, Raoul, and the other men."

"You have been happy in the woods, haven't you? Well, I am thankful for that. I should rejoice to feel that you are not leaving McGregor for good, but that some day you would come back over the old trail to take up my work."

Mr. Houston spoke earnestly.

"Do you know, Uncle Alf," Dick responded quite as earnestly, "that is what I should like better than anything else to do. I have thought of it over and over again. Every time

I've realized that some day I must go home to New York I've wished it was only to learn more, and then come back here. Of course I do not know enough now to be of any use in the woods, but I could study, and I would be willing to work hard. Do you think if I did, that some time I could be a forestry man like you?"

"Indeed I do. This spring when you return home I shall go with you to pay your father and mother a visit and if, after you've done a little more thinking, you still feel that you would like to fit yourself as a forester we can make plans about your studying the subject."

Dick's eyes glowed.

Then he said wistfully:

"I wish there was some way Raoul could go with us. He loves to learn and he has never had the chance to go to school, you know."

"Raoul?"

"Yes. I shall miss Raoul when I leave here," Dick added, slowly.

Mr. Houston was thoughtful.

"It might be done," he ventured at last. "The boy is a splendid manly fellow who certainly ought to have his chance. I never thought about it before. Mr. Dalton was much pleased with him when he saw him at Belleport this fall. Possibly he—he has no boy of his own—it might be—Mr. Houston broke off indefinitely.

"Oh, do you suppose he would help Raoul to go to school Do you think he would pay for his -"

"Come, come! Stop your castle building," laughed his uncle. "I do not suppose anything about it. But when we see Mr.

Dalton at the Belleport mills on our way out, I'll mention Raoul to him."

"Oh, Uncle Alf, if you only would! If Mr. Dalton would just get Raoul's clothes I am sure mother and father would let him come and stay with us so he could go to school with me. I'd help him with his lessons and I could buy books for him. I have some money," Dick concluded breathlessly.

"You'll have more money, too, Dick, when you leave McGregor," Mr. Houston announced impressively, watching the boy's face.

"More money!" repeated Dick, bewildered.

"Yes. Mr. Dalton wrote Harper, the scaler, about you. Harper is clerk for the camp during the winter, you know, and pays the crews. Mr. Dalton feels that carrying water, bringing wood, building fires, and doing errands as you have since last spring, deserve a salary."

"A salary? Money for me?" murmured Dick incredulously. "He wants to—to—pay me for that work? Why, Uncle Alf, I've only been trying to help Raoul and the men. I like to do it. I never thought of being paid. Besides, I ought to do some work because I've been so hungry and eaten so much."

Mr. Houston laughed heartily then said:

"All this was explained to Mr. Dalton, Dick, but he still thinks you have been faithful to your 'chores' and earned something. Harper has the check for you. I thought it would be no use to you here in the woods, so I asked him to hold it until you got ready to leave camp."

Dick was almost speechless.

After a pause he managed to say:

"Uncle Alf, I never had a check in all my life. I never had

the chance to earn money at home. What I've done here doesn't seem worth it."

"Well, evidently it has been worth it to Mr. Dalton. I didn't know you were to have it until Harper told me. He says you have put in some good regular work each morning and night helping Raoul about the camp. This has given Raoul time to do other things –"

"Time to fish some, I know that," interrupted Dick with a chuckle.

Mr. Houston joined in the chuckle.

"Yes, but it has really been a help too."

"I wanted to help."

Dick's mood shifted and he spoke earnestly.

Then he added:

"Well, if I have money I've really earned, Uncle Alf, there are some things I'd like to do. Christmas is nearly here and I'd like to send home some sort of presents—real presents I've earned—to father, mother, and Dr. Haughton. They've been mighty good to me. And I'd like to get some knives and things for the fellows at school. Then if I could only do something here for the men—I have been wanting to so much! Could I, do you think? Couldn't I get something sent from St. John—something we do not have in camp every day—something they'd like?"

Putting his hand on the shoulder of the eager boy Mr. Houston said:

"Well, you are not a millionaire, Dick. You can't present gifts to your family, the entire high school at home, and the whole Dalton force—much as I know you would like to. But you shall do some simple thing for the men in camp. I will think it over."

So as Christmas was still some weeks off Dick left the matter in his uncle's hands and threw himself into the life at McGregor more completely than ever.

He went on snow-shoes with Raoul, the cookee, who carried hot dinner to the crews at work in different parts of the woods, for at this busy season no one went back to the main camps for meals. It took too much time. Moreover, it was frequently too far. Therefore the food was brought to them by the cookee of each camp. He was a welcome sight to the hungry men, and even when afar off his coming was heralded by a jangling of the tin dippers which were strung together by their handles and which hung down his back. You may imagine how they clanked about him. The cookee brought a keg of salt beef, hardtack, and a big pot of coffee wrapped thickly in burlap that it might keep hot. Sometimes he brought a steaming ragout, or stew, which the men ate from tin basins.

Whenever Dick made these noontime rounds with Raoul he helped carry the food and dish it out.

Frequently, toward sunset, he went the circuit with the sprinkling carts which every night flooded the wood-roads so they would be smooth and icy the next day. The first time he went he exclaimed in surprise at finding hot water in the sprinkler.

"Why do you use hot water?" was his instant question.

"In zero weather what state would the water be in if we didn't start with it hot?" the teamster asked.

"Why—why—of course it would freeze before you had

He Helped Carry The Food

driven any distance. It wouldn't sprinkle at all. I might have known that if I'd thought."

Wherever Dick turned, new, interesting facts met his eye. Not a day passed but he learned some wonderful lesson not confined between the covers of a book.

"I'm surely going to be a forester some time, Uncle Alf," he reiterated.

So happy was he that almost before he realized it Christmas was little more than two weeks away.

"I've not forgotten about your sending some presents home, Dick," said Mr. Houston one day. "It seems to me that the very best things for your father and the fellows would be those of Little Toby's manufacture. Indian wares are not so common in New York as here. Toby has been making deerskin gloves, snow-shoes, moccasins, and bows and arrows during his leisure hours in camp. At Christmas time he sends them to St. John to be sold. Suppose, before they go, we look them over and see what he has."

"That is a splendid plan, Uncle Alf; but maybe they will cost too much."

"I do not think so. We will ask Toby."

So they made a trip to Sherwood to see the little Indian and, to Dick's delight, purchased presents for his father and the boys at home. To his mother he mailed a check from his very first earnings that she might buy a new gown.

Dick never felt so happy or so proud

"And the men here?" he asked after the large express package had gone out over the carry on Toby's shoulder.

"Oh, I've not forgotten them," Mr. Houston said. "Some of them will go out to Raven Brook to spend the day with their families; and others will be granted leave to go even as far as St. John; but many of them will be in camp. So I have ordered a lot of corn to pop and plenty of molasses, and we will have a candy-pull. You and I will give it together to all the lumbermen in the three camps. We can use big iron kettles swung over out-of-door fires, and we can cool the candy on the snow. Jake, Silver, Lutz, Raoul, and Harper will help us arrange it, I am sure. How does that please you?"

"Hurrah!" shouted Dick. "It is much better than anything I could think of."

"I'm glad you like it. Lutz will send to Raven Brook for the corn and molasses. The others will attend to getting together all the large iron kettles from the different camps. There is plenty of waste from the cutting which ought to be burned anyway, and we will take this opportunity to use the driest of it for our bonfires. I think we shall have quite a Christmas."

And sure enough they did!

Dear as were the home letters and the home packages; and strongly as his heart went back to those so far away, Dick spent at McGregor Camp the jolliest Christmas he had ever enjoyed.

In the morning the Sherwood and McGregor crews each built a huge snow fort and had a sham battle. Afterward Lutz served a hot dinner, with real mince pie, and there were races and games on the ice. Then when supper was finished the great iron kettles were swung over a crackling blaze of pitch-pine, and everybody shared in a most wonderful candy making.

The caverns of the forest were tinged far into their black depths with rosy, dancing glimmers from the fires; while overhead, in a sky sown with stars, darted the brilliant-hued Northern Lights.

It was a day long to be remembered!

"This certainly has been the very best Christmas I've ever had!" declared Dick as he rolled himself up in the blankets that night.

"I am sure some of your fun came from earning the money to buy the presents you gave away, Dick. Had you thought of that? A present never is a real present if somebody else just hands you the money to get it. The genuine gifts are those we work to make, or deny ourselves to buy."

"I'm sure of that, Uncle Alf. Hereafter I am always going to earn the money for the things I give away. It is twice as much fun!"

CHAPTER X

THE DRIVE

OWARD the middle of April, although the snow was still five feet deep in the woods and on the hill-sides, the ice on McGregor began to break up, letting the giant booms into the water; at once men set to work warping them across to the dam at the foot of the lake that they might be ready to tumble over the falls when the gate was lifted, and the drive started. The booming crews found their task no easy one, for McGregor was white with floating cakes of ice, through which they were forced to fight a channel.

While they were busy doing this the remaining river-men, who each year went down with Dalton and Company's Elk River Drive, and who had been at work in the meantime on outlying farms, began to straggle into camp. Picturesque figures they were in mackinaws, thick socks and high moccasins, and trousers hacked off just below the knee. Each man carried his dunnage bag strapped to his back and across it dangled heavy calked boots, copper-colored and cracked from exposure to sun and moisture. These boots were slashed at the toes to let out the water and often, too, they were even more slashed at the tops where the men had kept their tally of the drive. But beside this equipment every river-man carried his peavey or cant-dog—a long lance-like pole with a sharp hook in its tip. Dick learned that this peavey was the mainstay of the river-man. Not only did he use it to prod the timber along into the current, but he picked jams with it and also balanced himself when jauntily riding the logs in mid-stream. For a water-man to lose his peavey was a lasting disgrace. The advent of the driving crews proclaimed that at last cutting and hauling was at an end. Some of the teamsters who farmed through the spring and summer, and who were hired by Dalton and Company merely to help in getting out timber, left camp; and those who were to accompany the great drive along the shore trails waited patiently as did swampers, sledders, choppers, and the river-men themselves, for the rising of the water.

Mighty piles of logs stacked parallel with the stream bordered the river just below the sluice-gate, ready for breaking out.

For the second or third time the river-men rubbed tallow into their high boots and once more sharpened the inch spikes in the soles.

Lutz and Raoul in the meantime had been stocking the wangun—that unique little traveling kitchen built on a scow which always accompanies the drive, and is towed from shore by horses. During the three months or more that the crews would be at work getting the logs from McGregor down to Belleport this queer restaurant would always keep along with them. The wangun carried many delicacies not found on the regular camp menu.

"We have to feed the men well," Lutz explained to Dick. "We can't scrimp them on food when they are working so hard. We cook beans in a big tin wash-boiler—what do you think of that—and we serve from three to six potatoes to each man at a single meal."

"My goodness!" ejaculated Dick.

"Oh, a river-man gets up a great appetite," laughed Lutz, "So we give him five meals a day. He needs them, too. Often he is in the water up to his waist eighteen hours at a stretch."

"Do you mean that a river-man sleeps only six hours a day?" asked Dick, surprised.

"Six or seven hours is about all he gets during the rushing part of the drive. He has to keep at his job so long as there is a glimmer of light in the sky."

"Well, I don't wonder he needs five meals," said Dick.

So keen was the boy's interest in all this preparation that he was as eager as the driving crews for high water.

"Why, Dick, you are getting to be a genuine lumberman," declared Mr. Houston. "I expect that the next thing I know you will be dancing out onto the logs with a peavey."

Dick smiled.

"I'd like to, Uncle Alf. When do you think we can start the drive?"

"We can't tell. There is some ice in the Elk still, they say; but the small streams are clear, and can be kept so by crews sent ahead to break out channels and see they do not freeze over at night. The sun is getting hot, fortunately, so by the time we get down to the Elk most of the ice ought to be gone, unless we have a zero snap. If we should have severe cold after the drive is started, there would be a bad jam."

"What's a jam, Uncle Alf!"

"I'm afraid you will have many a chance to see before we get down with the logs," sighed Mr. Houston.

"Well, I wish we'd hurry and start."

"All we are anxious for now is plenty of water," his uncle said.

It proved they had not long to wait, for there were several warm days, followed by two of heavy rain. Early the next morning, while it was still drizzling, Dick was roused by a knock on the cabin door.

"The streams are down with a rush, Mr. Houston," shouted Jake. "We are going to break her out."

Dick and his uncle scrambled into their clothes.

There was little preparation to delay them, for their kit, packed for departure, had already been stowed aboard the wangun.

But once outside the cabin, all was confusion.

Figures dim in the darkness and the heavy mist hurried to and fro.

Dick could hardly be prevailed upon to stop at the cook-house for breakfast, and as it was he swallowed his meal whole. Then seizing a doughnut and a thick slice of cheese, he ran down to the Point, where his uncle, Jake, Silver, and the fore-men were talking.

"We'll keep back six crews here at the head of the stream," Silver said. "That will give us Peter's gang to go forward round the bend; crews Seven and Eight at the falls down-stream; and crew Nine with the wangun. The others can sluice the booms and come along later with the 'Mary Ann', getting into the current all logs that have been stranded on the edge of the river."

"What is the 'Mary Ann'?" queried Dick.

"Oh, here comes our question-box!" laughed Jake.

Dick grinned good-naturedly.

"I expect the box will be full and running over today," replied he.

"Well, I hope somebody will find time to answer you, lad," Jake remarked, glancing affectionately into the eager face looking up into his.

"I'll see to that," Mr. Houston declared promptly. "Dick must excuse you and Silver today. You have about all you can do. I am taking this trip down river for the very purpose of supplying answers to those interrogation points."

"Well then, Uncle Alf, please tell me what the 'Mary Ann' is," persisted Dick.

"The 'Mary Ann', my boy, is a small boat that follows the drive and carries provisions for the men at the rear, whose duty it is to see no logs are left behind. The rear of a drive is quite as important as the front, for it must be sent ahead while the water is high. In many streams it is possible to hurry it along by sending after it torrents of water from sluices. But here our men cannot resort to that method, and must simply keep the logs moving on as fast as possible, that the rear may not lag and fail to get down to the mill while the river is high."

Dick would have liked to ask other questions, but a sledge came creeping toward them through the melting snow. Onto this they were bundled and driven to the foot of the lake where they found the dam and the river bank black with lumbermen.

Jake took his stand on the dam while Silver, who was

to boss the front of the drive, made his way down to the river's edge. Here, with spiked shoes gripping the bark of a projecting log, he hovered over the water, peavey in hand, and addressed the men:

"Now after we break out the landings you fellows look lively. Keep the lumber moving in the current. No man is to take foolhardy risks, but he is expected to work for all he is worth. I do not need to ask you to do that, for you take as much pride in getting the drive down as I do. Just remember that if Dalton's timber does not get down these small streams before the water drops it will be tied up here until another spring and be a total loss to the company. Every inch of high water is worth dollars. Don't waste it. Make the most of it while it lasts. When you get into the Elk you will be sure of floating your timber and you can ease up the rush a little; but until you reach the Elk you've got to hustle. Now—break her out, boys!"

Raising his peavey, Silver skipped nimbly ashore just as the first great pile, with a thunder-like rumble, crashed into the stream.

The Elk River Drive was off!

There was a shout as the foam rose.

In another moment the logs were grinding against one another, whirling in the eddies, and wildly thrashing for space. The river seethed with dark struggling forms which sent up a dull, hollow cannonading as they struck in the chaos, and bounded off only to boom against others.

A score of river-men swarmed onto the moving mass, prodding the logs with their cant-dogs and aiming them into mid-stream. Dick caught his breath as he watched these fearless fellows. They leaped from one slippery trunk to another, running the length of each as carelessly as if they had solid earth beneath them, instead of a boiling yellow torrent. Suddenly Silver, who stood poising himself on a constantly turning log, waved his peavey to Jake, and shoving himself into the current, raced down the river and disappeared round the bend. One river-man after another shot into the rapids and away.

Then the next landing was cascaded into the water.

Once more there was spray, tumult, and a whirlpool of tossing timber.

Promptly another crew sprang forward and with pick-pole and peavey drove the logs out of shallow water into the current.

The reverberations from the bed of the stream were deafening.

Landing after landing thundered into the flood. In the angry white boil the logs seemed alive. Round and round they spun only to be swirled against other logs with a shock so powerful as to upend them in the stream.

The river-men worked like beavers to keep the mass moving and prevent a block, or jam.

With the help of a megaphone, Jake shouted orders from the dam above.

Dick, who stood beside him with his uncle, watched the scene with intermingled fear and delight. Why the dancing figures on the logs were not precipitated into the yellow turmoil raging all about them, he could not understand. But not a man seemed to think of danger, or of the lurching footing on which he stood. The work went on feverishly, recklessly.

Almost every pile had been fed into the stream by noon-day and then riders on fast horses were sent along the trails bordering the river, to give warning that the sluice was to be lifted, and the logs in the booms turned out and sent over the dam.

In the interim Dick and his uncle, together with the crews at hand, had time for some smoking stew served by the Sherwood cookee from the 'Mary Ann', moored some little way up the lake shore. The wangun had gone ahead to provide for those with the front of the drive. It was a hasty meal swallowed rather than eaten, and afterward came the climax of the day.

The great sluice holding back the water in McGregor Lake was lifted and with a rush of saffron foam beat down into the river bed, taking with it both logs and ice-cakes. A V-shaped boom had been constructed above the dam and into this enclosure the trees were fed, passing through its narrow point into the sluice. They shot over the falls as if directed from a rapid firing gun, while in the confusion and danger beneath the cataract, the river-men worked faster and faster to keep the drive moving.

Suddenly one log caught upon a boulder in the middle of the river and before it could be dislodged by a cant-hook another had upended against it. More logs, racing through the current, struck the barrier and piled up. Ice-cakes wedged in the crevices.

In an incredibly short time a heap of timber was firmly grounded midway from shore, and was rapidly becoming higher.

Jake shouted through his megaphone the moment the first trunk lodged, but his cries were useless.

"Get out there, men!" he screamed. "Keep off the logs coming down-stream, so they will clear the middle. Stave 'em off, I tell you! Stave 'em off!"

But it was too late. The giant travelers, spinning on their way, continued to be caught against those already fixed, and there they stuck.

A jam had formed!

Jake left his post on the end of the dam and went down to the river to be within closer range of the crews.

Twenty river-men were now fighting the jam, stabbing their cant-dogs first into one log and then into another in the hope of loosening it. They seemed to be playing a gigantic game of jack-straws.

"They'll have to blast her out, I'm afraid," Mr. Houston said to Dick. "No, Jake is calling for volunteers to pick the jam. It is very dangerous work, so we never compel men to go, for when the thing gives way it often goes so suddenly that the men are struck by the logs and knocked into the water, or swept down-stream. And yet I never knew of the call being made for help but about five times as many offered as were needed. See! Hear them shouting. There are at least twenty who want to go."

"Why do so many offer when it is dangerous?" asked Dick.

"Oh, they like to have the chance to show what they can do. These river-men have lots of pride. Who are those fellows Jake is singling out? Those first two are Sherwood men and there is Little Toby, too. Toby is like a water-sprite. See him run across those logs! He seems to bear a charmed life, for he has fallen into the rapids enough times to drown any ordinary man. But he always gets to shore all right, so you need not worry about him. Watch them work out there. They are picking off the top logs so to get down to the one that holds the entire jam. They call that one the key log. If they can get it free, the whole pile will go. Look, Dick, they are getting down to the heart of things. Some of the men are coming back to shore, for there is no need for so many now. But Toby is going to stay—you may be sure of that."

Dick watched, as the brave fellows tugged at the mass with their cant-dogs.

Then there was a cry from Toby.

All the men but himself rushed across the logs to land.

The jam rocked an instant.

Little Toby gave it one more wrench with his peavey.

Then there was a crash as the logs were torn asunder and swept down the current. A fountain of spray shot up. There was a gnashing of timber.

The men yelled and darted onto the floating tree-trunks.

But where was Little Toby?

"He's knocked into the river and drowned, Uncle Alf. It's horrible. Jake ought not to have let him go. Poor Toby! He was so good to me. Oh, Uncle Alf, I think it is awful to stand here and not do anything to save him."

Dick was entirely upset.

Just then, along the bank of the river near the bend, a dripping form came into sight.

It was Toby.

"Got carried down a ways," he grunted as he came nearer, "but she's clear."

Jake smiled.

"Well done, Toby!" was all he said.

And that was all that anybody said.

Dick, who had vaguely expected that Toby would be borne to the 'Mary Ann' on the shoulders of the river-men, was greatly disappointed. Even Mr. Houston was strangely unenthusiastic over the feat of the little Indian.

"It was wonderful! It was a grand thing to do, wasn't it, Uncle Alf?" cried Dick.

"Yes, my boy. It was both brave and wonderful. But remember that when a fellow becomes a river-man he undertakes such tasks as this constantly. He expects risks. Toby was brave, but there are any number of others who would gladly have done what he did; and there is scarcely a man on our crews but would have obeyed had he been ordered to go onto that jam. Give the glory to Toby, Dick, for he deserves it, but never forget to give equal praise to the rest of Dalton's river-men who take their lives in their hands every time they go down with a drive."

In the weeks following Dick had many a chance to prove the truth of his uncle's words. Such daring, such bravery, such uncomplaining devotion to work, such cheerful endurance of discomfort, he had never seen. It was a lesson not soon to be forgotten. And yet it was a joyous experience. The men sang their wild river songs as they tossed the logs free in the rapids. And they joked and laughed over every ducking they got. They were alert with the first streak of dawn and did not turn in so long as there was a single ray of light in the evening sky. Enduring bitter cold, wind, rain, they labored on. And the big drive went steadily forward, caught the Eagle crews with their logs above Sparville, and swept on down toward the Elk.

But with every mile they made Dick's heart became heavier; for he knew that as soon as he and his uncle reached the head of the Elk they were to leave the river and the men and take a cross-country ride to the nearest railroad. From there they would travel by train to Belleport to see Mr. Dalton, and the company's mighty mills, before they started for Dick's home in New York.

CHAPTER XI

THE MILL

ONE morning, when the rear of the drive was well on its way to the Elk, Mr. Houston said to Dick:

"I am sorry, boy, to wrench you away from the men here, but tomorrow—if all goes well—we shall reach Parkerstown; now at this point the McGregor River forms a loop, so that by riding half a day we can cover the land lying between the two parts of the stream, and easily catch the front of the drive, which has been delayed by cold weather. We have had a good trip down here with Jake. Now suppose we overtake Silver and the wangun, and go on to the head of the Elk with the vanguard. What do you say?"

"That's a fine plan, Uncle Alf," declared Dick. "I had no idea that we could reach the front so quickly."

"Usually we could not, but this year the crews have been obliged to blast out ice ahead, and have not made the rapid progress they expected. This is fortunate for us. Tomorrow, then, we will start from Parkerstown and overtake them. We can get fast horses there, and after we reach the river we can send them back."

"I hate to leave Jake," reflected Dick.

"I know. But you must leave him some time. Don't be downhearted about it. Remember, you are coming back."

The boy smiled.

"So I am! I had almost forgotten that."

Nevertheless it was a sad moment when early the next morning the big river boss came leaping across the logs to say good-bye to Mr. Houston and Dick.

"You'll not forget us, lad," he said. "And some day you will be coming home to McGregor, you see if you don't, knowing more about the trees than any of the rest of us. And then you'll set to work teaching me, just as I have tried to teach you."

"What an idea, Jake!" Dick ejaculated. "But I truly am coming back to the woods—no fooling. Be sure and wait until I come; don't ever go anywhere else, for McGregor without you would be no McGregor at all."

Jake rubbed his woolen mitten across his eyes.

"You'll see me standing with a fly on my rod," the lumberjack declared, attempting a laugh. "And I will have some baked beans buried down deep with plenty of hot coals round them, too, just the way you like them."

"It will be a long time before we get any more earth-baked beans," put in Mr. Houston. "Well, Jake, the season has been very satisfactory, and the drive has gone well. Thank you for all you have done for the boy and myself."

Mr. Houston took the great black mitten in his grasp.

"I don't want any thanks, sir. You know I like to work under you. And as for the boy—he's every inch a Houston. That's

The Big River Boss Came Leaping Across The Logs

the best thing I can say about him. Send him back to us some time, sir, and do not make it too long before he comes, either."

Two swift little ponies were now brought up which Dick and his uncle mounted.

"Never fear for the forest," Jake called after them as they rode off. "Silver and I will look after the baby trees. Good-bye."

He waved his cant-hook as he went back onto the logs, and Dick and Mr. Houston, returning his salute, and answering the cheers of the river-men who were in sight, turned into the cross-country trail.

Although the day was piercing the sun was warm, and as much of their way led through wooded country, they were not uncomfortable. It was afternoon, however, before they reached the crest of the hill from which the sinuous windings of the McGregor could be seen. Dick was the first to catch a glimpse of the silver thread.

"Oh, Uncle Alf," he shouted, "there is the river! How far away is it? Can we reach it before dark? Do you think we shall catch the drive?"

"We'll make it by sunset," Mr. Houston answered. "It is not so far off as it looks. We shall certainly overtake some part of the drive and if not, we can follow along the river trail until we do."

But Mr. Houston had calculated more accurately than he realized for, as they came down the hill into the valley, they could see the network of logs covered with moving figures. Gradually these figures resolved themselves into the familiar forms of men they knew. Then the wangun came into sight.

Dick could scarcely rein in his excitement when he saw Lutz and Raoul aboard.

"There they are, Uncle Alf! There they are! Look! They have spied us. Hurrah, Raoul! Raoul! Lutz!"

Two heads popped out of the cabin on the scow.

"It's Dick!" screamed Raoul.

Hatless and coatless the delighted cookee dropped his tin pans and darted to the river bank where the horses were standing.

The two riders were glad enough to slip out of the saddle.

Instantly a McGregor man rushed off the logs and catching the bridles of the tired ponies, led them to shelter in the Dalton shacks.

As for Dick, he left Mr. Houston to thaw his chilled fingers before the stove aboard the wangun while he and Raoul pranced back along the shore to find Silver. After a half-mile tramp they came upon the Canadian standing upright on a water-soaked log and drifting down-stream as he gave orders to the men behind him.

"Silver!" yelled Dick.

The river-man turned, stuck his cant-hook into the log he was riding, and taking off his soft felt hat swept Dick a bow so profound that he actually dipped up the foam which frothed about the tree-trunk on which he stood.

His fine teeth gleamed.

"Vive le roi!" he cried. "How does your majesty?"

"Oh, Silver, you'll fall off!" Dick cried.

But Raoul laughed.

"Not he! Why, Silver could dance a hornpipe for you right there in mid-stream if you wanted him to."

"Well, I don't!" declared Dick, terrified.

Silver, who evidently enjoyed his fright, executed a few

more gymnastics on his slippery perch and then, with sudden bound, jumped to a veteran log and over a score of others, reaching land.

"You're the best sight I've seen along this stream," he panted. "Where did you come from, and where's your uncle?"

Then, as they went on to the wangun, Dick told his story.

The McGregor men gave the travelers a royal welcome, and for two weeks Dick and Mr. Houston went along with the front of the drive, watching the blasting out of ice where the river was frozen; seeing a big jam blown up with dynamite; helping rescue three Sherwood men who were swept off a log into the rapids; and staving the wangun off the rocks near shore.

It was an exciting trip.

But alas, the drive constantly neared the head of the Elk— neared, and at last reached it!

Once more Dick was forced to say good-bye to the good friends whom he must leave to slowly wind their way down to Belleport.

He could hardly keep back the tears at parting from Raoul.

Silver, Lutz, Harper, and the McGregor men wrung his hand again and again!

"I'm surely coming back," was all the boy could say. "You all wait for me. And, Silver, take good care of Jake."

"Trust me for that, Dick. Good-bye, boy! It is like taking away the blue sky to have you go," Silver said.

For one instant he was grave; then out he danced onto the logs, and cutting every sort of caper, joined in the chorus of a song the river crews were singing. That was the last glimpse Dick had of him.

Raoul rode part way to the railroad with his friends, and then turned reluctantly to go back over the trail to the river alone.

But Dick and his uncle, feeling very conscious of their starched collars and city clothes, boarded the train and about noon the next day puffed into Belleport.

A little gray-haired man, who was pacing the platform as the engine pulled in, glanced up at the car window, then gave a quick nod.

"It's Mr. Dalton!" exclaimed Mr. Houston.

Nobody ever called Mr. Dalton anything but Mr. Dalton, Dick discovered. Well as his uncle knew the owner of the great mills it was never "Dalton," or "James" or "Jim." Dick could not imagine anyone ever calling Mr. Dalton "Jim."

"It seems as if he must have been Mr. Dalton even when he was a little boy, Uncle Alf. And yet he has the best smile I ever saw—even a better one than Silver's. His eyes, too, are very kind; and he shakes hands so—well—as if he was truly glad we'd come. But it must have been hard for Raoul to tell Mr. Dalton about the Loon Lake fire, for somehow you feel as if Mr. Dalton could never do anything mean or wrong himself."

"If he ever did do a mean thing it is so long ago, Dick, that neither he nor anyone else can remember it."

As Dick and his uncle were to be the guests of the Belleport mill owner during their stay in town, their luggage was sent to the house; they themselves went directly to the mills with Mr. Dalton.

Here, while Mr. Houston talked business, Dick was put in charge of a foreman who took him over the plant.

When he first entered the giant buildings the whirr of machinery was deafening.

"Why, this is even noisier than the drive!" he shouted in the ear of his conductor. "I thought that was bad enough, but this is dreadful. How do the workmen stand it?"

"Oh, they get used to it," shouted back the foreman. "They even get so they miss the noise when they do not hear it. But these large saws do make an awful racket, no mistake."

"I should say they did. How good the wood smells. The clutter of chips and sawdust on the floor looks so clean that it does not seem at all like dirt."

"It's a clean sort of dirt," returned his guide. "The men all like the work because it is so clean, but they have to be very careful of the great saws, of course. Now and then some of them get careless and we have an accident, but not often. The thing most to be dreaded is fire. We take every precaution against it. Not a man is allowed to smoke either in the mills or in the lumber yards. You'll notice there are signs everywhere warning the employees not to do it. I don't know what Mr. Dalton would do to a man whom he found smoking."

As it was so hard to talk above the roar of the mill, they walked upstairs in silence.

First Dick saw how the logs were brought in from the river on a sort of moving platform slanting up to the second story of the factory, and were there unloaded and stripped of bark, which was afterward dried, packed, and shipped to tanneries.

Next the slabs or curved faces of the timber were cut off and, together with smaller logs, utilized for shingles and laths.

As soon as the slabs were off, the square bolts of wood were run into machines that held them firmly while a band saw of flexible steel, passing over a wheel in the ceiling, cut the blocks into boards. Besides these band saws, there were gang saws which cut several boards at a time. And there were also large, round, revolving, circular saws, but the foreman explained to him that these made such a wide kerf, or bite, that they were very wasteful. Often the cut was a quarter of an inch wide, so that on every four boards a fifth was lost in sawdust. Therefore the band saw with its thinner blade was preferred in order to lessen the waste.

But in spite of all that could be done, there was much wood in the shape of slabs and edgings which could not be made use of—far more waste, in fact, than the mill could dispose of as fuel. So to avoid its accumulation hundreds of tons of useless pieces were yearly destroyed in large burners in the yards. This was the cheapest way, the foreman said, to get rid of them.

After the lumber was sawed, the boards were piled in the yards to be seasoned, being stacked crisscross so that the air could get between the layers. Some of the boards were kiln-dried, or exposed to heat, in order that they might not warp or crack when shipped for immediate use.

The lumber yards where the boards were piled stretched along the river ever so far.

"I should never find my way out if I once got lost here," laughed Dick.

"It is a pretty big place," the man returned. "All these piers that you see running out into the river belong to the Dalton Company too, and are often stacked with boards. Schooners come up alongside, anchor, are loaded with cargoes of different kinds of lumber, and then sail off to distant ports. Other timber which goes by rail is put aboard freight cars that come in on these tracks. And not only does the company make rough boards, but in those mills to our right we plane them so they are all ready to be used inside buildings. And just next to the planing mills are our wood-working factories, where boards are grooved so that their edges will fit together; and where we manufacture mouldings, door and window frames, blinds, and mantelpieces."

"Oh, I should like to see that. May we go in?" asked Dick.

"Certainly. It is very interesting if you have never seen it done."

So they went into another mill where the burr of planes and saws mingled with the ring of hammers. Everywhere Dick turned, seasoned timber was being transformed into some finished product. Great curls of thin shavings covered the floors and the entire factory, like the sawmills, was fragrant with the smell of freshly cut wood.

He could have spent a whole day here, but the foreman, who had work to superintend, now brought him back to Mr. Dalton's private office.

"Come in, Dick," called Mr. Houston in reply to his knock. "We were just speaking of you."

As Dick entered, Mr. Dalton looked at the boy sharply from under his heavy gray brows.

"Your uncle tells me you like our woods," he said. "Come, sit down and tell me all about it."

Dick seated himself in one of the slippery leather-covered office chairs.

"I was very much obliged to you for the money you paid me, Mr. Dalton," said he.

"Well, well. You were glad to have it, no doubt. Boys can always use pocket money. You earned it too, you know. Harper tells me you stuck faithfully to the chores, working like a little tiger. The Houstons always carry a thing through if they once set out to do it—it is a little way they have, and a very good way, too."

He smiled at Dick's uncle.

"But we'll talk no more about that money," he continued. "Tell me what you thought of the woods."

"You have the biggest and best woods I ever saw, and I never in my life had such a good time as I had there, Mr. Dalton. Some time I want to go back to McGregor. May I? I want to see the men, and find out what has become of the trees we have left to grow up. Uncle Alf says that if father and mother are willing he will help me to learn about the forest so some time I can do the sort of work he does."

Dick's eyes shone.

"Should you like to be a forester, Dick?" asked Mr. Dalton, still looking at him intently.

"I'd like it better than anything in the world!" burst out the boy.

"Do you think you would find it interesting, year after year, to spend your life in the woods taking care of the trees, and watching them grow up? You would not get tired of it, eh?"

"Oh, I'm sure I shouldn't. Why, Mr. Dalton, the forest is the very most interesting place to live—much nicer than being here at Belleport in these mills."

Dick heard, or thought he heard, a queer low chuckle from Mr. Dalton, but afterward he decided he must have been mistaken, for the gruff little mill owner did not smile.

Instead he went on with his questions.

"What about the cold weather, and the beans, and the salt pork?"

"I didn't mind any of those things," laughed Dick. "But yesterday roast chicken did taste good!"

A smile flickered in the eyes of the older man.

"Your uncle says that you and Raoul became great friends."

"Yes. I was sorry"—there was a catch in Dick's voice—"very sorry to leave Raoul."

"What should you say to my sending Raoul down to New York to study?"

Dick leaped from his chair.

"Oh, Mr. Dalton, could you—would you do it? I will promise to help him all I can, and I am quite sure mother would be willing that he should stay at our house."

"Your mother is willing," put in Mr. Houston, "for I have already written and asked her."

"Really? Oh, you're a trump, Uncle Alf! You know, Mr. Dalton, Raoul never had the chance to go to school, and yet you'd be surprised how much he knows. He has picked up some arithmetic from Harper, the scaler, and he does sums on pieces of board with a charred stick. One day I drew some maps in the sand, and the next day I found Raoul could draw them too, and drew them lots better than I did. He remembers everything you tell him. I am sure that if you sent him to New York to study he would work hard."

"I think he would," nodded Mr. Dalton. "The most difficult part of the plan would be to persuade his brother to part with him. Silver would die for Raoul, I'm convinced. The Loon Lake fire proved that. Of course it was not honest or fair of

Silver to take the blame for that disaster as he did, but his motive to shield Raoul was a noble one."

"The only way we could get Silver's consent would be to make him understand what an advantage it would be to Raoul to get an education," ventured Mr. Houston. "I am sure, too, it would make things easier if Silver realized that Raoul would be with Dick."

"And in your charge, Mr. Houston," added Mr. Dalton.

"Yes, Silver thinks Uncle Alf is about right—and so do I," proclaimed Dick with enthusiasm. "Besides, now that Silver and Jake are friends again, Silver won't miss Raoul so much, for Jake will cheer him up."

"Yes, that's so," assented Mr. Dalton. "Now my plan, Dick, would be to send Raoul to New York as soon as he arrives here with the drive. Your uncle can get a tutor for him immediately and we will push him ahead so that, if possible, he can enter college when you do. Afterward you can both attend some School of Forestry, and when you have finished you can come back to me and I will find work for you."

Dick was speechless.

Much as he wished to express his gratitude, his pleasure, his satisfaction, no words would come.

Perhaps Mr. Dalton was quite as well pleased that he said nothing. He patted the boy kindly on the shoulder and the interview ended. Although Dick and his uncle stayed three days in Belleport, the boy could never again get Mr. Dalton to mention the wonderful plan, and he began almost to fear that he had dreamed it.

But the morning the two travelers set out on their journey

to New York the small gray man shook Dick's hand with a firm grasp.

"Good-bye to you, Dick Sherman," he said. "Remember you and Raoul must be back here before long to help operate my forests."

And then Dick knew that his wish was no dream, but was really coming true!

CHAPTER XII

TEN YEARS AFTER

ID ever a boy receive such a welcome home as Dick Sherman?

Proudly his father measured shoulders with the tall son who over a year ago had been exiled to the woods; and as for his mother, she threw her arms about her boy and could not bear to let him out of her sight.

"Oh, we have missed you so, Dick! You will never know how much," she murmured again and again.

Dick's return even overshadowed the joy of having a visit from her brother, Mr. Houston, fond as she was of him!

Uncle Alf took it all good-naturedly.

"Cry over the lad all you want to, Elizabeth," he said. "I do not wonder the house has been lonely without him. But you must not fill him up with dainties the first thing, for he has not seen anything but beans, salt beef, and doughnuts for over a year, and you will make him ill."

Dick laughed.

"Oh, it was not quite so bad as that, Uncle Alf. We did have dried apple pie."

The day after his home-coming Dick went to see Dr. Haughton.

He dreaded the interview, but determined to have it over right away that he might know exactly the condition of his eyes. Then he could make his future plans.

When he walked into the oculist's office the doctor was busy and did not immediately recognize the lad, who had shot up several inches during the time he had been away. But no sooner did Dick speak than the old gentleman sprang forward with outstretched hand.

"Why, if it isn't our lumber-jack!" he exclaimed. "Well, well. What a giant you are! Trying to rival the Canadian pines, I'll be bound. Sit down, sit down. Now tell me all about the woods. Not the worst place in the world to live, eh?"

"Just about the best place, Dr. Haughton. Do you remember how broken up I was when I left this room last year? Well, I've blessed that balky nerve in my eye ever since, for if it had not given out I should have gone right on at school, and perhaps never have had this wonderful visit in the forest. Now I want you to examine my eyes again, and if they are not all right I am going straight back to McGregor. You need not fear to tell me this time if you find I cannot study, for I am half hoping I cannot. I'd like nothing better than to start for the woods now that I have seen father and mother. It seems so noisy, and so hard to breathe, here in New York."

"I know," returned Dr. Haughton, quickly. "After all, when we get down to the real man we find him still a savage. It would not take much to coax many of us back to sleeping under the open sky. Certainly it is much more like living than to pass our days in the rush which goes on about us here. And as for our little cooped-up houses—ridiculous, ridiculous! Well, we can't remedy it, I suppose. Now come here and we shall soon see whether you are destined this year for books or for more wood-chopping."

He proceeded at once to drag out microscopes, lenses, and many another contrivance that Dick did not understand.

Then in silence he applied one test after another.

At last he looked into Dick's face.

"It's Virgil and algebra this year, boy. I'm almost sorry for you, I declare I am, but I must be honest. There is not the shadow of trouble with that nerve now, so back you go to school, I'm afraid."

Dick chuckled.

After all, he was glad.

So he spent a week getting settled at home and seeing his friends. Then his father hired a tutor and he set about making up the year's work which he had lost. Before he was fairly underway, Raoul arrived.

It was a happy household that greeted him. Neither Mr. nor Mrs. Sherman could do enough for the young Canadian who had helped rescue their boy the night he was lost in Sherwood Forest, and who had since then been his almost constant companion. After Mr. Houston had taken Raoul to see the interesting sights of the city and thus made him more at home in his new surroundings, he found a tutor for him and began mapping out his studies. There was far too much foundation building which must be done for Raoul to keep pace with Dick for the present, but the Canadian was eager for study and so anxious to catch up with his friend that each day the distance between them lessened.

It was a proud moment when together he and Dick passed their entrance examinations to college. From Mr. Dalton in far-away Belleport came the wire:

"Well done. Keep at it. The forests are waiting for you!"

Through the long years of college work that followed both boys wrote constantly to Silver and Jake. They received in reply queer little messages. Sometimes it was a scrawl on a bit of birch-bark; sometimes a package of maple sugar; sometimes deerskin gloves of Little Toby's making. These things were precious, but they brought scant news of the life at camp, and more than once Raoul had an almost unconquerable longing to see McGregor and those he loved.

But the two clung resolutely to their studies taking, too, all the wholesome pleasures that came with college life. Raoul, who was of light, wiry build, won several cups for the high jump, while Dick went in for running and took medals for the hundred-yard dash. But they did not let athletics interfere with their work.

"We must store up all we can, Dick," said Raoul, "now that we have these books at hand. Remember that by and by the only library we shall have will be the one in our heads. I am memorizing all the good poetry I can so that I shall be able to repeat it to myself when I get to work in the woods. Besides, we must carry back all the interesting facts we can to Silver and Jake."

Their college days were so full of work and of happiness that four years passed almost before the boys realized it, and commencement was at hand. On class day Mr. and Mrs. Sherman and Mr. Houston had the satisfaction of seeing them graduate with a cum laude. The one cloud on the day was that Mr. Dalton, who had expected to come from Belleport, was too ill to do so. Instead he sent to Raoul a letter which almost made up for his absence. It was only a few lines saying that had the Canadian been his own son he could have been no prouder of him and he added:

"You have proved, Raoul, that you were indeed worthy of the opportunity given you. Never feel under obligations to me for your education. It was due you, and you have made the most of your chance."

Nevertheless, all was not yet learned.

In the fall the boys left the Sherman home and went west to a College of Forestry where they spent two years more in hard work. Afterward came a year of visits to large lumber camps in the West, the North, and the South, where they studied logging methods new to them.

Then at last both Mr. Houston and Mr. Dalton declared their education complete.

By this time Dick, who had stretched up until he was over six feet tall, was an alert businessman, quick to estimate situations, but still retaining that boyishness which had always won for him so many friends. Raoul, on the other hand, had become thoughtful, with cool, sound judgment beyond his years, and a dignity quite equaling that of Mr. Dalton himself.

And now, no sooner had the two boys finished their studies than they bade good-bye to Dick's parents, and started for Belleport. Raoul felt it his duty to report at once to Mr. Dalton, and as the young foresters had become the closest of friends, Dick was only too ready to accompany him.

How long ago it seemed to Raoul since he had come into Mr. Dalton's office to confess to the setting of the Loon Lake fire! With amusement, Dick pictured himself a small boy, sliding out of that great leather office chair, and the two chuckled aloud.

When they were shown in, Mr. Dalton sat in the very spot before his desk where he had sat ten years ago. He was still little and gray—a bit grayer, perhaps, than they had remembered him—but he was the same sharp-eyed, kindly man. For Dick, he had one of his hearty hand-shakes; for Raoul a hand-shake, too; then a lingering touch on the shoulder of the young Canadian.

"I am glad to see you, boys. You have done well! I'm proud of you."

It was only a few words, but in that moment the two were rewarded for all the self-denial which their training had demanded of them. Had Mr. Dalton given them each a gold medal it could have meant no more.

And then they sat down and talked and talked, pouring out with enthusiasm all the new lumbering methods they had seen; all their impressions of college life; all their college pranks—for Mr. Dalton would hear the pranks as well—and a multitude of questions about McGregor.

When they became too exhausted to say anything more Mr. Dalton drew from a drawer in his desk a bundle of maps.

"And now," said he," I wish to talk of your future. We have secured a long lease of the timber tract adjoining Sherwood, just over the ridge of Blue Mountain. It is a large reserve which we have been trying for years to get into our hands. It has wonderful pure forests of pine and also a clear waterway down to the Elk. All we need now is to open it up. So I am going to turn it over to you two young men to operate as you think best. Go up there with these maps and boundaries; explore the timber; locate the camps; oversee the building of them; pick your crews; hire your horses; make contracts for your machinery; and manage the forest conservatively so as to protect the trees and get a good annual yield of timber. The problem is yours—work it out."

Dick and Raoul gasped.

"You may take Silver and Jake along with you for council if you wish, for they have had experience, and their advice will therefore be useful. Perhaps, too, Mr. Houston would like to run up and see the new tract. Do not forget, however, that the venture is yours, and I shall hold you alone responsible."

"But we may make mistakes—we may lose money for you, Mr. Dalton," stammered Dick.

"Money isn't everything in this world. The company is not suffering for funds, neither am I. Your education will not be finished until you can put in practice what you have learned, and in order to do that you must have a clear field. This is what I am giving you. Go in, and do the best you can. You may make mistakes—I expect that—but two boys with your determination will never make a real failure, never fear. You can't fail!"

Once more Dick tried to speak.

"Mr. Dalton," he began, "Raoul and I will do our best. We cannot half thank you, sir -"

"There, there," broke in Mr. Dalton quickly but not unkindly," we'll have no more words about it. But before we close the subject entirely there is just one more thing which perhaps I would better say. Of course, I am not really an old gentleman yet, although I confess to a little rheumatism, and cannot deny I am almost as gray as a squirrel. The time is coming, however, when I shall be older, and then I may not feel like sticking as closely to work as I do now. When that time comes I want two able, well-trained young men to assume the management of these mills as well as of my forests, and be the acting Dalton and Company. Therefore, when you have your timber in good working condition, I shall send for each of you to serve an apprenticeship in these mills, that you may know the business from the peavey up; for who knows but I may choose to go traveling to Egypt or to California some fine day, or perhaps give up altogether. I shall then, you see, need someone in whose hands to leave the mills. Now you can be thinking it over. If you find you like the lumber business well enough to keep at it for life, here are places waiting for you. Do not answer now, think it over, think it over. Dick said long ago that he liked the woods better than the mills. Perhaps he might manage the forests and let Raoul take the mills. You boys talk it over."

Before either Dick or Raoul could say more he had swept them out of his office.

The next day, with the precious package of maps and boundaries, the two boys started for McGregor. The journey seemed never-ending. When at last they drew near the little tumble-down station of Raven Brook and caught sight of Jake and Silver on the platform, they could hardly wait for the train to come to a stop.

Ten years of outdoor life had swept lightly over the lumbermen who seemed scarcely a day older. But these same ten years had transformed the two boys into men.

Jake and Silver regarded them with astonishment, hardly knowing what to say. But a word or two, a jest, a hearty laugh and as if by magic the strangers became the "cookee" and the "question-box."

And then what fun it was to jolt in once more over the carry! And how jolly to find so many familiar faces at the camp! By the end of the day, it seemed to the two boys as if they had never been away from McGregor at all.

Then, in the quiet of the evening, before a crackling fire of hemlock, Dick and Raoul told the older men of their studies, their college life, their trips to other lumber camps. Afterward, they unfolded their future plans.

Jake fairly glowed with pride. As for Silver, he could only say:

"You've made good to Mr. Dalton, Raoul. Now do the best work you can. Do not disappoint him, lad. If you can only be worth enough to him to even up his loss in the Loon Lake fire I shall die satisfied."

"So shall I," murmured the boy softly.

There was a long pause. Then Dick said:

"Now tell us of McGregor, Silver. How is Uncle Alf's plan for saving the trees working out? Did the little ones grow up as he expected, so there should be a good yield each year? Or do you think Mr. Dalton has lost money, as you declared he would?"

Silver smiled.

"I'm always ready to admit when I'm wrong," he answered. "Your uncle's way is the only way to manage timber—I am convinced of it. By constantly protecting the trees we have raised as fine a forest as you would care to see, and we have sent a good drive down to Belleport each spring, too. Your uncle was right, Dick."

"Then if you really think so, you and Jake must come up to our new Sherwood Forest tract of timber and there help us to work out these same principles. Will you?"

"Surely we will. I reckon, though, that you and Raoul know more above the way to manage trees than we do," laughed Silver. "But we wouldn't miss having a share in your undertaking, would we, Jake? We're mighty proud of you boys. Good luck to you both!"

And there in the firelight, with a future fascinating in unsolved problems, let us leave Dick and Raoul and say with Silver:

"Good luck to you both!"